IN ME I TRUST
An Adult Choose Your Own Adventure Story

It's another day in the life of a hustler and you've got decisions to make. Are you going to hit the streets and get on your grind or will you screw around and trick it off?

You'll need to think fast and do the right thing - which doesn't necessarily mean the legal thing - if you're going to make it to the top and stay out of the hospital, prison, and the morgue.

With forty-six separate endings and hundreds of different paths to take to reach your destiny, no day will ever be the same. Bank robberies, drug deals, kidnapping, gun running, burglary, murder for hire, and more can lead to success or failure, it's your choice.

With pages full of sex, drugs, violence, federal agents, car chases, shootouts, double crosses and backstabbing, you know that the struggle is real and sometimes it feels good to be a gangster.

By D. Mann:

In Me I Trust
The Money Shot

In Me I Trust

D. Mann

Deviant Ways Publications
PO Box 94 – Montrose, MN 55363
www.DeviantWaysPublications.com

How To Read This Book

You will note that this book does not have page numbers. That is because it is not meant to be read one page after the other from beginning to end.

This book is divided into Scenes, beginning with Scene 1. At the end of each Scene are options and upon choosing an action you then go to that corresponding Scene. Continue this process until you reach The End.

For a new adventure, return to Scene 1 and make different choices.

Refer to the FAQ at the end of the book for more information about this choose your own adventure story.

In Me I Trust

It's been one of those weeks - fuck that, it's been one of those years. You lost your job - well, all three of them, but they weren't shit and you were only working to appease your probation officer, which you don't need to do anymore. You lost your girl - well, both of them; the first walked when she caught you cheating and the second you kicked to the curb when you caught her fooling around on you. And now you've walked outside to find your ride has been totaled by some piece of shit hit and run driver in the middle of the night. You stopped paying insurance two months ago, so now you're really fucked. If you had a dog that ran away they could write a fucking country song about your life.

At least I'm free, you tell yourself, having been out of the joint now for almost two years if you don't count the halfway house. But you expected yourself to be having a lot more fun with your freedom than this. That's not to say you haven't had some good times since you've been out, but mostly it's been a grind and it's wearing you down.

> If you decide that it's five o'clock somewhere and go to the bar, go to Scene 2.
> If you really want to get fucked up, go to Scene 3.
> If you think you'd better start looking for a job, go to Scene 4.

You make your way to Shaggy's, a local bar that's filled with a dozen or so people sitting at the bar or small tables. You recognize the daytime bartender, but don't know his name which is fine because he doesn't know yours either. You order a drink and look around at the crowd seeing a few familiar faces, but no one special. You realize that you're kind of getting sick of the same old scene, kind of like you're getting sick of your same old life. What's that they say: SSDD. Same shit, different day.

Turning back to face the bar you finish your drink and order another. You look at yourself in the mirror, not entirely disappointed with what you see, but you ask yourself what's it going to take for something to change. You can't keep living like this; well you can, but you sure as fuck don't want to. Something else catches your eye in the mirror: a woman at a small table behind you who seems to keep looking your way.

As you turn around on your bar stool you see your bro Chaz walk through the front door. You look to the table where the cute redhead is sitting and she gives you a smile. You've seen her before - pretty sure her name is Mandy or Maggie or Mallory - but you've never talked to her.

> If you walk over to the redhead's table, go to Scene 5.
> If you wave your bro Chaz over to the bar, go to Scene 6.

You make a phone call and thirty minutes later you're sitting in Trevon's living room getting high as a kite.

"'Ere," you say as you pass the blunt to one of the other five people sitting around on the couch, recliner and loveseat. You know two of the guys and one of the girls, but the couple on the loveseat you've never seen before.

"How do you know T?" you ask the unfamiliar guy.

Trevon speaks up for his guest. "That's Maggot. Don't you remember him? He was in the joint with us?"

You shake your head and say, "I would have remembered somebody named 'Maggot'."

"Yeah, yeah. Maybe he left before you got there."

The plump, plain looking girl on the couch next to you puts her hand on your thigh. Her name is Veronica or Vera or Virginia, something like that, and you think you might have fucked her once but you were too high or drunk to remember. "I'm glad you're not in prison anymore," she says and gives you a homely smile.

"Me, too," you reply. She squeezes your thigh but you're not sure if you're high enough or drunk enough to want to get with her. "Hey, T, you got anything stronger?" you ask.

"Sorry, man, alls I got is weed right now."

"We've got some shit at our place," Maggot tells you. His girl sitting beside him is pretty hot and smiles at you.

The homely girl beside you stands up and grabs your arm and says, "Come with me for a minute. I want to show you something."

> If you go with the pleasantly plump girl, go to Scene 7.
> If you leave with Maggot and his girl, go to Scene 8.

You hop on a bus and take it downtown to the Workforce Center where you got two of your last three jobs. After standing in line for half an hour and waiting in the lobby for another hour, your name is finally called and you're led through a doorway to a small cubicle. You sit in a plastic chair across the desk from an older dark skinned woman with graying hair. She greets you warmly with a smile and asks what sort of work you're looking for.

"Anything that pays a hundred thou a year," you tell her.

"You and me both," she laughs. "Can I ask what is the reason you lost your last two jobs that you got through us?"

"I didn't lose them, I know right where they're at," you say jokingly. When she doesn't laugh you say, "Well the last one the manager was a --" you stop yourself before saying 'fucking asshole' and mend it to, "he was disrespectful. And the one before that just didn't fit for me." The manager at that one was cool, but everyone else was a fucking asshole.

"Okay," the helpful lady says, "you don't have any negative remarks on your file, so we're still willing to assist you." She prints out a page and hands it to you and tells you that the place on the page is taking applications until three o'clock. "Good luck."

You thank her and walk back to the lobby where you see standing in line your bro Tony that was in the joint with you. "I haven't seen you for a minute," he says. "Wanna go get a beer or something and catch up?"

> If you tell him you've got to go to a job interview, go to Scene 9.
> If you blow off the job interview and get a drink with Tony, go to Scene 10.

"Hi," you say as you walk over to her table.

"Hi yourself," she says with a flirty smile. "I've been watching you."

"I know. I was starting to feel like I was under surveillance."

"You think I'm a cop?" she asks and then looks you up and down. "Maybe I need to frisk you for weapons."

"Maybe you'd find one."

She laughs and tells you her name is Noelle. You tell her your name. From where you're standing beside the table looking down at her in her chair, you can see about five miles of cleavage. You feel your weapon begin to load.

"Wanna get out of here?" Noelle asks you.

Before you answer, Chaz grabs your arm. "I need to talk to you. I've got something big."

> If you ask Noelle to excuse you so you can talk to Chaz, go to Scene 6.
> If you blow Chaz off so you can show Noelle something big, go
   to Scene 11.

You and Chaz sit at the bar and get drinks. "I've been looking to catch up with you," Chaz says.

"I've got a phone. You've got a phone. Not too difficult," you reply.

He shakes his head. "No bro, this is a big score I'm putting together. Nothing that can be talked about over the phone."

"Since when did you start putting together jobs?"

"I've got some inside info that's golden. I'm talking six figures. But I need someone with balls."

"I've still got mine," you tell him. You and Chaz had done a couple of small licks back in the day, but nothing of this caliber. "How many people are involved?"

"Just one other, a driver. You and I will be the inside guys."

"Inside where?"

"A bank."

"Seriously? There's not much money in banks when you compare the risk to reward ratio."

"There is when you hit the vault, which is what we're going to do," Chaz says.

"With just two of us inside? So you have the weapons and equipment?" You realize you're stalling because you're not so sure about doing a bank job. That's looking at serious fed time if caught and you're not about to be serving any more time anywhere. You order another drink and then look over your shoulder. The redhead is gone. Damn!

"This is going down tomorrow," Chaz tells you. "So I need to know right now if you're in or out."

> If you're in, go to Scene 12.
> If you're out, go to Scene 13.

You follow the girl down the hallway, watching her bubble butt sway from side to side, and tell yourself that maybe she's not that bad. She pulls you into the small apartment bathroom, shuts and locks the door. She presses her warm, soft body against yours and asks you, "How come you don't ever answer my texts? I thought we had fun after that party a couple weeks ago. Didn't you?"

"Um, yeah," you say, still unsure what her name even is.

"It's obvious you like me," she says as she rubs herself against your hardening groin. Of course it's hard not to like any girl who rubbed against your crotch. You're still not sure if you want to get freaky with her right here in the bathroom.

"So, uh, you had something you wanted to show me?" you say.

She gives you a sly smile. "I just said that so you'd come with me. But I did want to tell you to watch out for Maggot and his girl Alicia, they're bad news."

"So you're not going to show me anything?"

"What do you want to see?" she asks. She licks her lips as she watches your eyes look her up and down. Playfully she says, "I'll show you mine if you show me yours."

A minute later your pants and underwear are around your knees and your cock is jutting out in front of you like a flag pole. She smiles hungrily as she slides her pants down and turns to show you her plump, bare ass. "What do you want to do, big boy?"

> If you point to your crotch and say, "It's not going to suck itself," go to Scene 14.
> If you bend her over the counter and take her from behind, go to Scene 15.
> If you tell her you'd like to take her on a proper date, go to Scene 16.

"Maybe some other time," you tell the plain girl, and in your head think: when I'm really desperate. You leave with Maggot and his girl, whose name you're told is Alicia. You're riding in the back of an Audi, nothing too flashy though it's brand new and still has that new car smell.

"What did you do time for?" Maggot asks you as he drives cautiously and keeps it under the speed limit.

"Which time?" you say. "Some robberies, assaults, distribution. What about you?"

"Possession and sales of methamphetamine. I gave them five years and that's all they get."

"I hear that."

"You got a woman?" Alicia asks you.

"When I want one," you tell her.

Alicia looks at her man and says to him, "We should fix him up with Deedee."

Maggot laughs. "Deedee would eat him up."

You don't think that sounds all bad.

They have a small, unassuming home in the suburbs and you're hanging out at a center island in the kitchen when Maggot sets a small gym bag down. He opens it and pulls out a stuffed Ziploc baggie of blue and yellow crystals. You note a few more similar packages of meth in the Reebok bag. Alicia produces a glass pipe and a blue lighter, puts a couple shards in the bubble end and heats it up to a fine white smoke. The pipe gets passed around.

"I've got an offer for you," Maggot says.

> If you want to listen to his offer, go to Scene 17.
> If you want to jump him and steal his shit, go to Scene 18.
> If you tell him you're not interested in the dope game, go to Scene 19.

You take the bus to the east side of town and then have to walk two blocks until you get to a large warehouse with the name Happy's Vending and Gumball Machines. You walk through an open garage door and the place is crammed to the ceiling with crates and boxes of practically every type of candy available. There are about twenty men and women in red and white striped shirts with Happy's Vending logo of a deranged looking clown above the left breast pocket.

A girl wearing pink Spandex pants and licking a sucker smiles as she walks by and you ask her where the office is. She tells you and you don't hear a word of it as your attention is focused on her tongue savoring the green sucker. You've got a sucker for her, you think as she walks off. You head in the general direction she pointed, walking past workers filling up red and white striped vans with boxes of candy.

You step through a door that leads to a hallway and drowns out the sound of the warehouse. There are a few doors along the hallway and you go to the first one with a sign on that says 'Private' and figure it could be the office. What you find instead are large bins on wheels, at least ten of them, two feet square, filled with all denominations of coins. There's a table with coin wrapping machines and a caged shelf, currently unlocked, with hundreds of boxes of rolled coins.

"Can I help you?" a man asks from the hallway, obviously returning from the bathroom. You tell him you're looking for the office and he points you two doors down before he goes into the money counting room and locks the door.

> If you go to the office so you can see about working here, go to
  Scene 20.
> If you decide to leave so you can come back and rob the place,
  go to Scene 21.

"When did you get out?" you ask Tony as the two of you kick it at a sports bar a couple of streets over.

"Nine days ago, and it fucking sucks. I'm at this fucking halfway house with a bunch of snitches and cho-mo's and my case manager is riding my ass about a job, which is why I was in line at the bullshit Workforce Center." Tony takes a swig from the Heineken bottle in front of him.

"Don't they give you a breathalyzer when you go back to the halfway house?" you ask.

"Fuck them. I ain't going back."

"What are you going to do?"

"As soon as I saw you, man, I knew it was a sign," Tony says and downs the rest of his beer. He orders another. "I don't want to make no ten or fifteen dollars an hour only to give it to the corrupt government for taxes and then half of what I have left goes to the halfway house for court fees and restitution. Screw all that. I want to make some real money."

"Like what are you thinking?" you ask.

"I'm thinking you've been out a couple of years, you've got to have some shit on lock. Let me in on some of your action. I'm down for whatever: heists, moving product, kidnapping, I don't give a fuck!"

You don't have the heart to tell him that your life and attitude is almost as miserable as his. Tony has less than five dollars to his name, so you pay for his drinks and you two leave the bar.

> If you decide to band with Tony and commit some crime, go to Scene 22.
> If you choose to part company and go your own way, go to Scene 23.
> If you decide to cheer Tony up by bringing him to a strip club, go to Scene 24.

"Not today, Chaz," you tell him as you slip your arm around Noelle's waist and head for the door. Chaz is always talking about some great scam or heist he has in the works but almost never pans out.

"Aw man," he says behind you. "Whatever happened to bro's before ho's?"

"I'm on the new shit," you reply. "Holes before poles."

As soon as you and Noelle make it to her town house you're both naked and your pole is before her hole. She has a petite body with a little extra around the hips and huge, natural tits with a sprinkling of freckles across them. You slide into her juicy warmth and the little airstrip she has proves she's a natural redhead.

Noelle's fingernails scrape across your back as you thrust into her again and again. You grab one of her titties and bring it to your mouth, swirling your tongue around the nipple. She goes wild with ecstasy, screaming out as she wraps her legs across your lower back. The sound of your slapping bodies increases and quickens as she cries out, "More! More! More!" until you've given her all you've got, exploding your hot cream inside her.

As you lie in bed talking and lightly touching each other she tells you about her new job working at a jewelry store. This of course piques your interest and you casually ask questions of pertinence to your career as a criminal, which Noelle seems to know nothing about. You ask about silent alarms.

"Mr. Horwitz says they're useless. He keeps a .44 Magnum behind the counter and has foiled two robberies, even shot a guy once."

You start to formulate a plan. But first you fuck Noelle again, real good.

> If you proposition Noelle to help you rob the jewelry store, go to Scene 25.
> If you decide to get one of your buddies to help you, go to Scene 22.

The next morning you're sitting in a stolen Escalade with Chaz and Rocco, the driver. All three of you are wearing identical Donald Trump masks and oversized navy blue suits that cover the body armor you're wearing. The SUV is idling in a supermarket parking lot across from United Trust Bank and you're watching the comings and goings from the bank awaiting Chaz's cue.

You notice a set of blinds on one of the large front windows closing and then opening, closing, opening.

"That's it. Let's go!" Chaz says.

Rocco pulls out of the parking lot, crosses the four lane street, and pulls up to the front doors of the bank. While he does that Chaz explains that the signal meant the manager and loan officer had left for their lunch break and only a teller and head teller remained inside.

"Which one gave you the inside tip?" you ask.

"What difference does that make?" Chaz asks as he checks his Tec-9 submachine gun. He hides it under the suit coat.

You do the same with the .357 Magnum you're carrying while saying, "It makes a big difference. You don't think her little signal is going to be seen when they review the security footage?"

"Fuck it, we're here," Chaz says and then looks at you. "Are we going to do this?"

You figure it's too late to wonder how big of a mistake it was to get involved with Chaz. The guy is always scheming but thinks he's a lot smarter than he really is. But it's too late to back out now.

> You and Chaz rush into the bank. Go to Scene 26.

"Thanks, but no thanks," you tell Chaz.

He looks a little shocked and says, "What, have you gone soft since you got out?"

"Fuck you. It's not about me being soft, it's about people being caught doing big bank jobs because there's almost always an inside person and that inside person almost always folds or gets caught in a lie under police interrogation."

"So we'll kill her," Chaz says.

"Kill who?"

"Who do you think? The person on the inside. That plugs the leak. Are you in?"

"Since when did you become so hardcore?" you ask.

"Since I got tired of getting kicked by the world and the fucking system. I decided I'm ready to kick back and do whatever it takes to get on top. And that means bigger jobs and bigger risks."

You can't really argue with this and you, too, are sick of being worn down by the day to day grind. It would certainly add some high intensity fun and excitement to the day. The only thing that still holds you back a little is that you've only done some small jobs with Chaz, nothing as heavy as this and so you're not sure how he'll act.

"What do you say, man, are you in?" Chaz asks.

> If you say "Yes," go to Scene 12.
> If you say "No," go to Scene 27.

She smiles widely and then puts that smile to use as she wraps it around the head of your cock while dropping to her knees. Her mouth is wet and warm as she slathers your stiff prick with her saliva. She grips her hands around the base of your shaft, twisting and turning while her head bobs back and forth. She takes you all the way into her throat, removing one of her hands to fondle your balls as she emits little gagging sounds.

You brace a hand on the bathroom counter as your other hand digs into her hair at the back of her head. She looks up at you admiringly as she sucks and slurps your throbbing cock. You feel yourself nearing eruption as you fuck her mouth.

You pull out and tell her to stand up. She does as she's told and you turn her around and bend her over the counter.

> Go to Scene 15.

You push her up against the counter and slip your dick into her from behind. She gasps as you grab her thick hips and plunge into her. Your balls slap against her as you thrust back and forth and her pussy's tight and warm.

"Oh yeah, baby," she moans as she braces herself with her hands against the mirror on the wall.

You lift up her shirt and pull down her bra, feeling her jiggling boobs. You reach around and clasp them in your hands, watching the two of you in the mirror's image as you continue to fuck her fast and furiously.

"Ooh, right there, right there," she tells you as you pinch her nipples and bounce against her ass like a jackrabbit. "Don't stop!" she cries as her pussy convulses against you and her eyes roll back in her head.

"Oh yeah, here I come," you groan.

"Don't come," she pants, "in me." She lets out a yelp as your cock pounds in her. "I'm not on birth control."

You can't hold it any longer and you almost think, fuck her, she can take the morning after pill. But what if she doesn't - do you really want to take the chance of this woman having your kid?

At the last second you pull out and slap your hand to your cock and shoot your load all over her ass and back.

You two clean up and put your clothes back on and return to the living room. She gives you her number that you pretend to put into your phone; hell, you still don't even remember what her name is.

Maggot and his girl get up to leave and ask you if you want to join them. The plain, chubby girl you just fucked asks if you want to go to her place.

> If you leave with Maggot and his girl, go to Scene 8.
> If you say you have shit to do and leave by yourself, go to Scene 28.

You realize you must be pretty fucking high, and probably so is this girl whose name you can't even remember. Not to mention you don't have any condoms on you and if this girl pulls down her pants this quick for you, how many other guys is she fucking on a whim?

You pull your pants back up and decide to try to be a gentleman. "How about I take you out to dinner tonight?"

"You're fucking kidding, right?" she says with her eyebrows raised and mouth hanging open. "My pussy is staring you in the face and you want to talk about going on a date? What are you, some sort of faggot?" She tugs up her pants angrily.

"That's not it," you say. "You seem like a nice girl and I--"

"Go fuck yourself!" she says and storms out of the bathroom. You hear the apartment door slam shut and some muted laughter from the living room.

"Damn, bro, what did you do to piss her off?" Trevon asks you.

You shrug your shoulders and say, "Some people just aren't happy when they can't have what they want."

Maggot and his girl have already left and it's only you, Trevon and one of his friends left in the living room.

"'Ere," Trevon says, offering you the blunt between his fingers.

"No thanks," you reply. "I'm going to head out. I'll catch you on the flip side."

"Right on," Trevon says as you leave the apartment.

> If you decide to get a drink at a bar, go to Scene 2.
> If you choose to take a walk to clear your head, go to Scene 28.

"I've got a deal going down but one of my drivers just got popped. I need you to pick up a shipment for me tonight. I'll pay you five grand," Maggot says.

"A shipment of what?" you ask.

"What the fuck do you think? Meth."

"How much would I be picking up?"

"What difference does it make? What's with all the questions? I'm just asking you to do a simple task: drive to point A, pick up package B, and return it to point C."

"If it's so easy, why don't you just do it?"

"Because that's what I'm paying you to do." Maggot pats his girl Alicia's fine ass and says to her, "Is this guy kinda slow or what?"

"Be nice, Maggot," she tells him. "He's just a little scared because he doesn't know who you are."

"I'm not scared," you say.

"Okay, fine," Maggot says, throwing his hands in the air. "Ten thousand. Only a complete fool would pass that up."

You take another hit on the pipe when it's passed to you and you're impressed with the quality of his shit and that it has very little aftertaste. You're pretty sure you won't be sleeping for a couple of days.

"What do you say, can I count on you?" Maggot asks.

> If you tell him you'll make the pickup, go to Scene 29.
> If you tell him you don't want to get involved with drugs, go to
   Scene 19.

You take another hit on the pipe and you're feeling no pain - too bad Maggot won't be feeling the same in a couple of seconds. You eye the gym bag sitting on the counter a couple feet away and figure there must be at least a hundred grand of product in it. You grasp the glass pipe in a fist, the stem of the pipe sticking out a couple inches, and jam it into one of Maggot's eyes.

There's a sickening popping sound and the bubble at the end of the pipe quickly fills up with blood and eye juices.

Maggot screams and grabs at the glass sticking out of his eye socket.

You grab the gym bag from the counter and run for the nearest doorway.

Alicia yanks open a kitchen drawer in front of her and grabs a chrome .45.

You reach the door to the garage and then hear the loud boom of the handgun, drowning out Maggot's screaming. The impact of the heavy slug hitting your back propels you hard against the door. You slide to the floor leaving a streak of blood down the door.

"Sonofabitch!" you hear Maggot yell and then footsteps approach you. The footsteps and his voice sound like he's in a tunnel a mile long. He's standing above you, his woman next to him holding the smoking gun.

"You think you're going to steal from me?" Maggot says. "In my own house? And you don't have a gun? You stupid fuck!"

You see Maggot's foot coming much too fast at your head.

> Go to Scene 30.

After getting nice and high you tell Maggot that you appreciate his hospitality but you're not interested in getting into the dope game. "There's too many snitches and the feds are giving out too much time," you tell him.

"The money makes it worth the risk," he replies. "And the perks are nice, too," he says and squeezes Alicia's ass.

You offer to pay him for smoking you up but he doesn't want your money.

"I like you, that you're straight up with me," Maggot says. "What are you doing tomorrow evening?"

"After smoking this, I'm sure I'll still be up." You both laugh.

Maggot looks at his sexy girl Alicia and then at you. "I was supposed to accompany Alicia to an event tomorrow evening but something came up and I have to fly out of town. How would you feel about escorting my girl?"

"Maggot, that's not necessary," Alicia says and then looks over at you. "I'm sure he has better things to do than want to babysit me."

Actually, you don't and you contemplate spending the evening with the drug dealer's smoking hot woman. I mean what could go wrong, right? Of course the answer to that, in your life, is lots, lots could go wrong. But it's a tough offer to refuse looking at her perky breasts in her tight shirt, so tight you can see a hint of nipple outline. But then do you really want to spend an evening with something you're pretty sure you can't have?

> If you accept his offer to take out Alicia, go to Scene 31.
> If you tell Maggot you've already got other plans, go to Scene 32.

"Do you have a driver's license?" the bald guy with the peanut shaped head asks you from the other side of his desk. You tell him you do. "Have you ever been arrested for a DWI?"

"A DWI? Nope, never been arrested for that," you say. A dozen other things, you think to yourself, but never a DWI.

Your mind keeps wandering back to the money counting room and how lax the security in this business is. But then you think of the nightmare it would be trying to get all those coins out of the building and how many hundreds or even thousands of pounds the haul would weigh. You tell yourself that sometimes knowing when to forego an opportunity is the right thing to do.

The little, bald manager is talking away about vehicles, uniforms, policy and pay, but mostly you hear blah, blah, blah. "How about we put you on a route tomorrow with Tamara?"

"Sure," you say, hoping that Tamara is the one who likes green suckers.

"Excellent! Glad to have you aboard. Let me get you a couple of company shirts," he says and darts out of the office. He returns with two red and white striped shirts and then you're making your way back to the bus stop.

You stop off at a little restaurant near your place and think about the new job and a little glad you've got something positive to look forward to tomorrow.

At home you flip on the TV intending to get a good night's rest before your first day on the job. Your cell phone buzzes and it's a text from your homie LT, it reads: 'I know where Ramone is!!!'

> If you ignore the text and go to sleep so you can make it to work,
  go to Scene 33.
> If you text back, 'Come get me now!', go to Scene 34.

You figure why work some place for weeks only to earn a few hundred dollars when you can work for a few hours and make a few thousand. You slowly make your way out, noting that the only security evident are contact sensors on the doors and garage doors but no motion sensors in the building and no cameras. The perimeter of the warehouse is surrounded by a chain link fence topped with three strands of barbed wire slanted outwards. Along one side of the warehouse are dumpsters and stacks of pallets. There are other warehouse businesses in the area but no homes or apartments.

As you take the bus home you contemplate whether you should call a friend to help you out; it never hurts to have backup or at least a lookout. But that would mean splitting the profits, which you don't really want to do. Besides, the job should be pretty easy, in and out, piece of cake.

You return after dark, taking the last bus of the night that runs by the warehouse district. You're wearing dark blue jeans, a dark green flannel shirt and a black ball cap. On your back is a backpack with a few necessary tools. All of the warehouse businesses are closed up and there's no traffic or people around. It almost feels like a ghost town.

As you near your target you check one last time to make sure the coast is clear and then quickly move to the large gate that's secured with a heavy chain. You pull the bolt cutters from your backpack and slice through the chain and it falls to the asphalt. And that's when you hear the sound of someone rushing fast towards you. Your heart races and you hold the bolt cutters like a baseball bat over your head before realizing that it's not a person coming at you, but a guard dog.

A big, black and brown Rottweiler lunges at you, but luckily he's on the other side of the fence. He barks and growls at you, none too happy that you're there.

> If you decide to open the gate and take on the dog with the bolt
  cutters, go to Scene 35.
> If you decide to trick the dog, go to Scene 36.

You meet up with Tony the next day and tell him about some info you have collected about a jewelry store. "The place doesn't have any silent alarms but the owner does keep a gun under the counter," you tell him.

"So his one gun against our two?" Tony asks. "My math tells me that we win that war."

"Especially if we get the drop on him. You'll need to do all the talking, though. One of the employees knows me and could recognize my voice."

"No problem. It's not like there's much to say."

"This a robbery. Nobody fucking move!" Tony screams as the two of you rush into The Golden Scepter jewelry store the next day. Both of you are wearing ski masks and holding menacing looking handguns. The small jewelry store is located in a strip mall between a mattress store and a weight loss center. Inside the establishment are three employees behind the counter and one customer, all of them with terrified looks on their faces.

"Don't even think about it, old man!" Tony says when he sees one of the employees moving his hand toward the counter. Tony pulls a ball peen hammer from his waistband and begins smashing the glass display cases and you're right behind him scooping up all of the goods into a gym bag. The whole action doesn't take more than thirty seconds.

Tony looks at you and asks, "Should we hit the safe?"

The plan was to get in and get out, but you know that jewelers always keep their biggest diamonds and most expensive pieces in the safe.

> If you nod to Tony to hit the safe, go to Scene 37.
> If you take what you've got and you and Tony leave, go to Scene 38.

After a couple drinks with Tony you decide he's got too much negative energy and that's the last thing in the world that you need. Not to mention that he just got out of the joint and you don't want to feel responsible for him fucking up and going back.

"Hey, bro," you say to him, "I think you should go back to the Workforce Center and see if they can hook you up. They've helped me with a couple of jobs."

"Are you kidding? Tell me you're kidding," he says. "You're seriously giving me the brush off?"

"Sorry, man, I just don't have anything going on right now. Look, I was at the same place you were, hoping to find work. I wish you the best."

"Fuck you and your wishes," Tony says. "I always knew you weren't about shit." He flips you off and heads off down the street.

Now you're really glad you didn't team up with him and his negative ass. The ungrateful bastard didn't even thank you for the drinks you bought him. You think to yourself that they need to start sending a better class of people to prison because most of the guys you've met there aren't fit to wash your car. That is, if your car wasn't sitting wrecked in front of your home.

As you walk down the street your cell phone vibrates. It's a text from your ex, Gina, saying she'd really like to see you. She was a sweet piece of ass but you cut her off about a month ago when you found out she was fucking around with other dudes. It didn't matter that you, too, were fucking around - you took care of her and spent a lot of money on the bitch, so she had no right to do you like that. But that doesn't mean the pussy's not still real good.

> If you decide to hook up with your ex, go to Scene 27.
> If you ignore her text and to the bar, go to Scene 2.

"Now this is what I'm talking about!" Tony says as you pay admission for both of you and you step inside the dark atmosphere of Velvet, one of the better strip clubs downtown. Hip hop pulses through the club's speakers and a dozen beautiful girls in lingerie are working the floor. On the stage is a topless platinum blonde whose surgically enhanced tits seem to defy gravity.

You sit down at a small table near the stage and a big boobed black girl in a tight corset takes your drink orders and returns a few minutes later with your purchases that Tony makes no attempt to pay for. Before either of you get your first sips in, two scantily clad ladies ask if they can join you.

"Hell yeah you can join us," Tony says and the girls happily take seats in your laps. After not more than a minute of chit chat the girls are asking if you'd like lap dances.

"Does the pope shit in the woods?" Tony exclaims, which the strippers take to mean yes.

Tops come off and crotches are grinded against. Twice Tony tries to cup one of the dancer's breast and each time she tactfully pushes his head away. After the third attempt, a floor manager in a suit approaches and informs Tony to please keep his hands to himself. The dancer faces Tony as the song nears to an end and he wraps his mouth around one of her small titties. The floor manager rushes over as the dancer pushes his head away and jumps back.

"What! I kept my hands to myself," Tony cries.

The two of you are escorted out of the club, but not before you have to pay for both yours and Tony's lap dances.

You decide hanging with Tony is too much on your pockets and you don't really care for his attitude, so you tell him goodbye and walk off on your own.

> Go to Scene 28.

It turns out that Noelle actually does know that you have a criminal past and she thinks it's kind of sexy. "I like bad boys," she says as the two of you lie naked in bed and her fingers tickle your balls.

"Are you a bad girl?" you ask as your hand moves up and down her back and over her ass.

"If I am, are you going to spank me?"

"If you are then you can have anything you want."

"Ooh, I like the sound of that. Ooh, and I like that," she says as your fingers slide up and down the crack of her ass. She begins to stroke your hardening member as she asks you, "How bad to I have to be?"

You tell her.

The next day you walk into The Golden Scepter jewelry store wearing a disguise of fedora, sunglasses and a fake beard. Behind the counters are two women, one of which is Noelle, and an old guy who must be the owner, Mr. Horwitz. You pull out your gun and declare, "This is a robbery!"

You're a little surprised to see how fast the owner whips his gun out from underneath the counter. It's a big, scary looking chrome revolver, much bigger than your gun, and pointing right at your head. "Drop your gun!" the old man says.

"No, you drop your gun," you say calmly as you step closer and turn your gun on him. The man's eyes grow wide and then there's a loud CLICK as he pulls the trigger. Your heart stops for a moment but then you're thankful that Noelle did her part and removed the bullets from the gun. You hit the guy in the side of the head and take away his piece. Then you throw a gym bag to the ladies and tell them to fill it up. Two minutes later you make a clean getaway.

> Go to Scene 39.

As soon as you and Chaz burst through the lobby doors of United Trust Bank, you're both yelling and waving your guns.

"Hands in the air!"

"This is a robbery!"

"Nobody moves, nobody gets hurt!"

On the other side of the counter are two female bank employees, one in her forties and the other about half her age. Three customers are also in the bank, two guys and a woman, all of whom have their hands up. As Chaz jumps over the counter you keep watch over the customers and the front door. "Get on the floor!" you tell them, keeping a close eye on one of the guys that looks like he could be in the military.

Chaz throws a duffel bag to the older employee and then points his gun at her as he grabs the younger lady by the hair. "To the vault!" he demands and the three of them disappear to a back room.

Out of the corner of your eye you see one of the men's hands moving towards his pocket. "Hey!" you yell and rush to him, stomping on his wrist. He screams in pain and says something about his cell phone vibrating. You point your gun at the other guy who is watching you intently.

"Freeze! Police!" you hear from behind you. "Drop your gun now!" You look over your shoulder to see the female customer up on one knee and pointing a small handgun at you she pulled from her ankle holster.

Chaz comes out of the back using the younger lady as a shield and pointing his gun at the older employee. He tells the undercover cop to drop her gun or he'll kill the employees. When she doesn't comply, Chaz shoots the older employee in the head. The cop swings her gun towards Chaz.

> If you shoot the cop, go to Scene 40.

> If you try to kick the gun out of the cop's hand, go to Scene 41.

You know it's not the smartest thing to go and hook up with your ex, but you're a pro at doing lots of things that aren't the smartest for you. She's been texting you off and on and right now you wouldn't mind a little familiar pussy - the girl does know how to use that body to make you feel good.

No sooner are you through Gina's apartment door and you two are tearing each other's clothes off. She's a sexy Puerto Rican who never said no to anything sexual, which unfortunately meant not saying no to other guys when she was supposed to be with you, which is why she's now an ex. But that makes no difference at this moment as you have her curled up on her back on the couch, her ankles touching her ears, your cock ramming in and out of her, your balls slapping against her ass.

She's orgasmed twice, but you're not ready to blow your wad yet. Your cock is slick with her juices as you pull it out of her tight pussy and slowly slip it into her even tighter asshole. Gina gasps and moans in delight as her hands grasp her ass cheeks and pulls them even farther apart. You push all the way into her until you're nuzzling your groin against her ass cheeks while your hands squeeze and fondle her titties. Within minutes you're riding in and out of her like a jackhammer and she's screaming your name as you spurt your hot cum into her.

"You sure do know how to fuck me," Gina says as you two sit back on the couch.

"So do you," you say, still salty that she had to go and cheat on you. You really thought she was down for you, a ride or die type chick who had no qualms about your criminal background and current activities.

"I've got some info from this guy I know," she tells you.

"Some guy you're fucking?"

"You were fucking around, too. Do you want to hear the info or not?"

> If you tell her, "Sure, whatever," go to Scene 42.
> If you say "No thanks" and leave, go to Scene 28.

You're thankful it's still nice outside as you walk the streets alone and try to clear your head. You think about the wild and crazy ride that has been your life and you're a little disappointed that you don't have more to show for it. Most people your age are married, having kids, working the nine-to-five grind, and living their lives to everyone else's standards. You're thankful you're not them.

You've always been independent and lived life your way, according to your own set of rules. Of course, that has meant some time behind bars but don't do the crime if you can't do the time. You're not trying to go back to prison any time soon though, so you've been careful with your criminal activity and who you choose to associate with.

You fuck around with your phone, checking your text messages and social media accounts. There's a house party going on tonight and it looks like quite a few people you know will be there. Your cousin Will has sent you a private message asking if you want to help him move tonight, and you know he's not talking about furniture. There are also two text messages that spark a little interest in you. The first is from your homie LT who sent: 'I know where Ramone is!!!' The other is from this rich girl you fuck with sometimes, but she always has a lot of drama in her life; Ashley sent you: 'Call me ASAP!'

> If you decide to go to the house party, go to Scene 43.
> If you reply to Will that you'll help him out, go to Scene 44.
> If you text LT and tell him to come pick you up, go to Scene 34.
> If you text Ashley and ask her what's up, go to Scene 45.

You tell Maggot you'll make the pickup for him and he says, "'Atta boy. I knew you had some sense in that head of yours." He puts your phone number in his cell and then tosses you a set of keys. "Take the Range Rover parked in back. I'll text you the time and place later this evening when it's ready to go."

"And my ten grand?" you ask.

"Get a load of this fuckin' guy," Maggot says to Alicia. He looks hard at you and says, "Bring back my truck and my drugs and you get paid. Fail to return with both of those and you get buried."

As you drive away you think about how much you really dislike that smug bastard. Maybe you'll have to teach him a lesson in humility someday. You picture his hot piece of ass Alicia in your mind and figure she's just with him because of the money. Well someday you plan to be rolling in the dough like that too and this could be the start, maybe do a few more runs for Maggot and then roll that money into something bigger.

You swing by a pizza place and grab a bite to eat as you await the text for directions. 'U-Stor-It, near the river, locker #270. Combination is 24-7-28. Ready now' comes the text message on your phone. As you drive over there you wonder if there's a gate code or something but upon arriving are surprised to find the gate open.

You locate locker #270 which happens to be a ten foot by ten foot room and inside is a green suitcase the size of an airline carry on. You peek inside and see what you expect: bags of methamphetamine. You toss the suitcase in the Range Rover.

As soon as you leave the U-Stor-It premises you notice two quickly approaching vehicles. Flashing red and blue lights appear and they hit their sirens.

> If you pull over, go to Scene 46.
> If you make a run for it, go to Scene 47.

You hear the sound of water and feel the cool night air on your face. Slowly, painfully, you open your eyes as you feel your body being jostled and lifted and you see a metal railing. You try to cry out but there's duct tape over your mouth. You try to move your body but it's bound tight with rope or tape.

You see the river eighty feet below but there's nothing you can do as you're pushed over the side of the bridge. The wind whistles by your ears as you fall head first and your neck snaps when you hit the water.

Your lifeless body floats with the fishes.

THE END

The next evening a black Lincoln Town Car shows up at your place and the driver opens the back door for you. You get in to find Alicia in a sexy, golden evening gown that's so tight it looks like it could have been painted on. The front is low cut, showing lots of cleavage, and the dress is slit up the side and showing a mile of leg.

"Wow," you say and try to keep your tongue from hanging out. She smiles and says, "Thanks. You know, you really don't have to do this if you don't want to. I don't even know why Maggot brought it up."

"It's cool," you say, trying to keep your eyes on her hazel green eyes but which keep tumbling down to her breasts. "So, where are we going?"

The two of you are driven to a fundraising event at a local college that turns out to be boring as fuck. It's a good thing you're still high from the day before or you would have probably fallen asleep on your feet. At one point she's leading you back to the car and you don't know if the event is over or what.

"You didn't look like you were enjoying yourself," she says.

"I'm sorry. Was it that obvious?"

She nods her head and smiles. "Wanna do something fun?" Alicia asks.

"Sure."

"Have you ever tried molly?" she asks and shows you two pills in her hand.

"Only when I fuck," you tell her.

She lifts her hand between the two of you and asks, "So do you want to take one?"

> If you take the pill, go to Scene 48.
> If you think it best not to try to fuck Maggot's girl, go to Scene 49.

You leave Maggot's place high as fuck, but that doesn't mean your mind isn't scheming and calculating angles. You figure it's not a good idea to be alone with Alicia because you're sure you'd try to put the moves on her and no matter how that went it could turn out bad.

On the other hand, Maggot told you that he's going out of town tomorrow night and Alicia has some event to attend which tells you that their small suburban home will be empty, and it didn't look like they had any sort of security system. You're not the type of person who rips off friends, but seeing as you just met them you certainly wouldn't call them friends.

Of course if Maggot somehow found out it was you who ripped him off, there could be serious consequences. On the plus side, it's not like he can call the cops. You wonder what else of value might also be in the house and start thinking of ways you might be able to get inside.

> If you choose to burglarize Maggot's home tomorrow, go to Scene 50.
> If you decide you want nothing more to do with Maggot, go to Scene 51.

The first day of work is just that: work. The worker you're teamed up with, Tamara, isn't the green sucker licker but rather a heavyset lady in her forties who reminds you of one of your elementary school teachers. She's constantly telling you what to do and how to do it and then correcting your every little error. By three o'clock you arrive back at the Happy's Vending warehouse and then spend the last two hours stocking the van for tomorrow's deliveries.

Most of the employees are all leaving around the same time and you catch a glimpse of the girl you'd seen yesterday working the sucker. She's got on the company red and white striped shirt as all the employees wear and a pair of yellow pants so tight you can tell she's not wearing any panties. As if hypnotized you follow behind her from a distance, your eyes glued to her ass and entranced with its every move. It's like a lollipop that needs to be unwrapped and licked until you get to the center.

"Hey!" a deep voice yells at you.

You look up to see that the sexy worker you were following has stopped beside a pimped out purple Impala on chrome rims. Standing beside her is a short Mexican in chinos, a wife beater and a blue bandana that practically covers his eyes. "You eyeing my woman, Holmes?" he asks and takes a step towards you.

"Hard not to with an ass like that," you reply.

"Aw shit! I know you, fool," he says. "You did time with my brother, Roberto. I'm Lil Taco."

You remember his brother, but not him. "How's Roberto?"

"He's dead. Hey man, come party with us. My brother had mad props for you."

> If you're too tired and would rather rest up for work tomorrow, go to Scene 52.
> If you get in the car with Lil Taco and his sexy girl, go to Scene 53.

Your homie LT is as dark as an eight ball and probably as big as a pool table. He picks you up in his Suburban and the first thing you say is, "Where is he?"

"Good to see you, too, Homeslice," LT says.

"I'm sorry, man. It's just that this motherfucker Ramone has been ducking me for so long."

"You need to relax before you give yourself a heart attack or ulcer or some shit. I told you we'd find him, didn't I?"

"Yeah, I know. Thanks. How've you been?"

"I'm smooth as silk," LT tells you. "I've got this fine new woman on my team and she's a nasty freak. I think I'm gonna marry this one."

"Bullshit. Marriage, really?"

"When you find the very right one, you don't want to let that go. I think she's it."

"Wow," you say with genuine surprise, "I don't think I've ever heard you talk like this."

"That's because I've never found anyone like this."

You arrive outside of a bar called Blinky's and LT sends a text on his phone and gets an immediate response. "My girl Keesha is working the bar, says Ramone is still here, sitting in a back booth. How do you want to do this?"

> If you go inside to confront Ramone, go to Scene 54.
> If you sit in the Suburban and wait for Ramone to come out, go
  to Scene 55.

You pull open the gate and swing the bolt cutters at the dog's head. You're surprised at how quick and agile the dog is. The beast snaps at your arm and you jerk backwards, narrowly missing his snapping jaws. The Rottweiler lunges again as you're bringing the bolt cutters around for another swing.

You feel the dog's sharp teeth tear into the meat of your thigh and you scream out in pain. You bring the bolt cutters down like a sledgehammer but the dog jerks you off balance and you hit the dog with a mere glancing blow that doesn't even phase the animal. The pain is excruciating as the dog tears into your flesh and muscle and he's jerking his head trying to shake you like a ragdoll.

Once again you swing the bolt cutters, connecting with the dog's midsection. The animal yelps and lets go of your leg; you can feel your warm blood filling your pant leg and running down your thigh. The dog growls and circles around you and you hold the bolt cutters ready to swing. You try to hobble back towards the gate which the dog had pulled you more than ten feet from.

Quickly you glance over your shoulder to see how close you are to getting out. The dog makes a running leap for your throat. Instinctively you react by bringing up your arm to block the attack and the beast clamps onto your arm. You hear the bones of your forearm crunch between the Rottweiler's powerful jaws. You scream and yell as you beat on the dog with the bolt cutters until he lets go.

You make it to the gate but the dog grabs onto your good leg, right by the calf. You jab the bolt cutters at him but miss and take out a chunk of your own leg. "Fuck!" you scream and grab the gate and bash it against the dog's head until he lets go of you.

You're bleeding all over the place as you pick up the chain and wrap it around the gate so the guard dog can't get out. The dog continues barking and growling as you painfully limp away.

> Go to Scene 56.

You recall a few blocks before getting off the bus there was a 24-hour McDonald's. You secure the gate with the chain as the dog snarls and barks at you. Fifteen minutes later you're back with a bag of hamburgers. You unwrap one and offer it halfway through the fence, but the dog ignores it and stays focused on you. You push the burger all the way through the chain link fence and then step back. The dog sniffs the food and then quickly takes it and eats it greedily. You approach the fence with another burger and the animal stops growling and barking long enough to eat the next hamburger you offer.

You remove the chain from the gate and then toss a handful of hamburgers a dozen feet away as you open the gate just wide enough for the dog and keeping your body behind the chain link. The dog glances at you but runs to the hamburgers. You dart inside the gate and close it behind you, securing it with the chain.

Along the side of the warehouse you stack the wooden pallets atop the dumpster and climb onto the flat rooftop. You go to the area where you remember the offices are; taking a crowbar from your backpack you pry a large fan contraption loose enabling you to drop down into the building.

For the next four hours you load numerous boxes of quarters and dimes from the money counting room to the back of one of the red and white striped vans. Your arms and back are sore after loading at least a hundred boxes which you estimate to be close to $15,000. You take a break and munch on some candy as you contemplate whether you should continue to work to get the rolls of nickels and pennies as well, which will probably be another few thousand dollars. You didn't think it would take as long as it did and you're not sure how much more weight the van can handle.

> If you decide to leave with the loot you have, go to Scene 57.
> If you choose to load up every last penny, go to Scene 58.

"Come on, old man," Tony says to the owner and waves his gun at him toward the back room. You go to the counter and grab the large, chrome .44 Magnum revolver. You watch the other two employees and the customer, all females, as you hear Tony in the back room prodding the owner to open the safe.

There's a jingle of bells that surprises you as you realize someone is coming through the front door. The middle aged man walking in is oblivious to the robbery as he is adamantly tapping on his smart phone. You lower your voice to hopefully make it unrecognizable to the female employee you know: "Hey dumbass!"

The man looks up and freezes for an instant, seeing you at the far end of the counter holding a gun in each hand, a gym bag looped over your shoulder, a black ski mask and gloves and the terrified victims. An instant later the man is turning and running for the door. "Stop!" you yell as you level the .44 on him.

He doesn't stop. He reaches for the door.

> If you shoot him, go to Scene 59.
> If you let him go, go to Scene 60.

The original plan was a smash and grab robbery, a quick in and out, and you know what can happen if you deviate from a good plan. You shake your head at Tony and head for the door but still keeping your eye, and gun, on everyone in the store. Tony's right behind you as you rush out of The Golden Scepter and jump into the stolen Cadillac in the parking lot. Tony's in the driver's seat and the car's wheels chirp as it takes off.

You see the owner of the jewelry store standing on the sidewalk, his big gun in hand. Tony sees him, too, and brings up his gun but you tell him to chill. "We don't want any bloodshed because that'll bring too much heat," you say.

The owner of the store doesn't fire his weapon because there are too many cars and people at the strip mall parking lot. You get away clean and a half mile away Tony turns into an apartment complex where you dump the stolen car and get into Tony's piece of shit Ford Explorer that barely starts.

"The first thing I'm doing is getting a new ride," Tony says and you look forward to getting your own ride fixed. "How much do you think we got?" he asks you.

"Hard to say. The watch case had half a dozen Rolexes between ten and fifty thousand and I know someone who'll pay us about a third of their value. We've got quite a bit of gold and some nice diamonds, too. I'm sure our take home will be over six figures."

"Fuck yeah!" Tony says and gives you a high five. "That went so smooth, we should do a few more."

"Maybe someday, but right now we're good for a little while. Let's unload this stuff and have us a little celebration."

"Fuck yeah!"

THE END

It's almost two weeks before you see Noelle again, which you both knew would be necessary in case the employees were suspected of an inside job. The police could find no such evidence and assumed Mr. Horwitz's gun must have malfunctioned or in all the excitement he only thought he'd pulled the trigger.

Noelle meets you downtown where you've gotten a hotel suite with a Jacuzzi tub in it. No sooner is she through the door and the two of you are naked, pawing at each other like sex starved maniacs. Her pussy is hot and moist as you fuck her from behind bent over a lounge chair near a window that overlooks the city. She clings onto the chair for dear life as your cock rams back and forth. She cries out in ecstasy as one of your hands reaches around and fondles her breasts while your other hand is on her pussy and stimulating her clit while you fuck her into multiple orgasms before exploding inside her.

"That was so good," Noelle says as you two lounge in the hot bubbly water facing each other, your feet playing with each other's genitals.

"The sex or the robbery?" you ask.

"Both! Oh my god, when you were robbing the jewelry store my nipples were so hard I had to keep from smiling. It was so thrilling and I kept thinking how it must feel to be on the other side of the gun."

"It's a rush, for sure, but during the robbery you don't think much about it. The adrenaline rush is better than any drug."

"I want to do it!"

"Sex or robbery?"

"Both," Noelle says as she slides her body atop yours.

> If you take Noelle on a robbery, go to Scene 61.
> If you take Noelle on a vacation, go to Scene 62.

Flame bursts forth from the barrel of the gun in your hand and a split second later blood and brain matter bursts forth from the other side of the cop's head. Before her body even hits the ground you swing your gun back towards the two men. Neither of them has moved.

Chaz comes from behind the teller counter, his arm still around the neck of the young teller, a gun in one hand and the duffel bag of money in the other. He looks at the dead cop with the entrance hole in her temple and says, "Nice shot."

"Why did you shoot the head teller?" you ask.

"She was the loose end we don't need to worry about now."

"What are you doing with this one?" you ask, looking at the terrified young teller.

"She's our insurance policy to make sure we get away. Come on!"

He tosses you the bag of money and you race for the door. You get outside and can hear sirens. The teller tries to pull away from Chaz's grasp but he yanks her into the waiting Escalade. You hop in the back seat, the young lady between you and Chaz, and Rocco slams the accelerator down and peels out of the lot.

"Fuck! How'd they get on us so fast?" you ask as you see a cop car blazing behind you, its lights and sirens blaring.

"Shit happens," Chaz says.

"What do you want to do?" Rocco asks from the driver's seat. "Do you want me to try to ditch them or we can all jump out on foot and head different directions."

"Or we can try to take them out," Chaz says.

> If you tell Rocco to keep driving and try to lose them, go to Scene 63.
> If you decide you should split up and confuse the cops, go to Scene 64.
> If you tell Rocco to stop so you can battle the police, go to Scene 65.

You think shooting a cop to not be a good idea because it will bring too much heat if you guys get away, and death sentences if you get caught. You snap your leg out at the officer's hand holding the gun. She senses your movement and instinctively rolls to the floor and fires her weapon at you. Red hot fire erupts in your leg as a .38 slug pierces your thigh. You scream out in pain and fall to the ground.

Both you and Chaz shoot at the undercover officer but she has rolled behind a desk.

"Look out!" Chaz yells and then you feel a body land on you from behind. It's the military looking dude who has jumped you and is trying to get the gun out of your hand. You head butt him in the face and his nose explodes in a red mist. There's more gunfire in the bank, Chaz and the officer taking shots at each other.

The civilian playing hero still has a grip on your gun arm. You knee him in the groin, yank the gun free and shove it under his chin, pulling the trigger. The top of his head explodes like a bursting watermelon, blood and brain matter spraying out of him like a fountain.

There's no more gunfire coming from the desk, so either the cop is dead or out of bullets. Chaz jumps over the counter with the duffel bag of money and helps you up and you both run for the lobby doors. You can hear sirens outside. Suddenly the Escalade burns rubber out from in front of the bank and takes off.

"Hey!" Chaz yells, letting you go as he runs for the door. You fall to the floor and yell at Chaz but he keeps going. You fire your gun at him, hitting him in the ass. As he tumbles against the lobby doors you see police cars screeching to a halt out front.

You and Chaz raise your guns up, whether to point at each other or at the police makes little difference. Either way you're dead.

THE END

The info Gina tells you turns out to be quite interesting, and there's no doubt in your mind that she's fucking the guy she tells you about. His name is Lloyd and he works for a courier service in the city and twice a month the guy picks up a package from a dental office in the suburbs and drops it off at a rundown house in the projects.

"What's in the package?" you ask.

"I don't know. But Lloyd says the package is insured for six figures."

"And you have no idea what it is?"

"What the fuck did I just say?"

"So what do you want me to do?"

"You're the criminal, figure it out. Get whatever it is and we'll split it fifty-fifty."

You raise your eyebrows. "Fifty-fifty? Are you going to help me?"

"I just did - I told you about it."

"You think that entitles you to half? All you get is a finder's fee, maybe twenty percent."

"Fuck that! You can't even do it if I don't tell you where he is," Gina says angrily. "Either I'm in for half or forget about it."

"I'll have to think about it," you tell her.

"Whatever," she says and gets up from the couch. You grab her arm and pull her back to you. "What do you want?" she says.

"For you to help me think," you reply with a smile and she feels your hardness rising up between you two. She smiles and presses her body against yours.

"So you'll do it?"

> If you fuck her and tell her "Yes," go to Scene 66.
> If you fuck her and tell her "No," go to Scene 67.

You arrive at the house party a little after ten. You tried to get a ride from a couple people you knew going there, but everyone had excuses so you just took the bus. You tell yourself you really need to make some money so you can get your car fixed.

The two story house belongs to Brandi and her guy Eddie. You've been to a couple parties here in the past. There are cars parked up and down the street and at least a couple dozen people inside with another dozen in the backyard where there's a gross, green algae covered in-ground pool.

You're greeted by a number of people as you walk through the house that is bumping loud with music. There are blunts being smoked in the living room, lines being snorted in a back bedroom and shots being taken in the kitchen. There's a lot of laughter and loud talking, but you realize your mind isn't really on party mode and you're starting to wonder why you even came here tonight. And what's more, you can't leave until you find a ride because there are no more busses this late.

There's a lady about your age leaning against the wall by herself holding a bottle of Corona that she doesn't seem too interested in. She's got wavy, sandy blonde hair, an average build, wearing jeans and a sweater. A couple times you catch her looking at you so you approach her and ask, "Having a good time?"

"Not really," she answers. "How about you?"

"The same." You find out her name is Beth and you two have quite a bit in common. She says she's thinking of blowing the party because she's just not feeling it. You ask her if you can get a ride.

"Sure," she says, "where to?"

> If you ask her to coffee, go to Scene 68.
> If you tell her to take you home, go to Scene 70.
> If you have her drop you off at your cousin Will's, go to Scene 44.

"I thought you'd never get here," your cousin Will says to you. He's a big, bulky guy with a bald head, tattoos all over his body, and still wears denim and leather from his days in a biker gang. He runs solo now but still deals with them and anyone else with money. "I need you to go to Dragon's Breath and make a pick up for me."

"What am I picking up?"

"Molly. Hurry up, Stryker is freaking out," Will says as he throws you the keys to a 1984 GMC conversion van with wall to wall carpeting and a bed in back.

Stryker is the owner and head artist at the tattoo parlor known as Dragon's Breath and he doesn't look freaked out when you walk into the place. He does look like a freak with his green spiked Mohawk, tribal tattoos on the sides of his skull, large pieces of metal pierced through his ears, eyebrows, nose and nipples, and ink of every shape, size and color over every inch of skin.

"Hey," you say with a nod of your head as he looks up from his task. He's bent over a woman laid back in a chair, her gym shorts pulled down to her knees exposing a clean shaven pussy. Stryker's right hand is holding her flesh taut while the tattoo gun in his left hand continues working on an old fashioned diner sign that reads "24 HOUR EATS" with an arrow pointing at her pussy.

"On the couch in the back," Stryker tells you and bends back down to his work.

You walk through a small hallway to a lounge area in back where you've done many drugs with Stryker, Will and friends. You wonder how much molly you're picking up and then you see: about a hundred and fifteen pounds worth. On the couch is a petite female whose hands and ankles are bound with rope and a piece of duct tape over her mouth. She looks at you with frightened eyes.

"Not again," you say to yourself.

> Go to Scene 70.

"I said call me, not text me, dumbass," Ashley yells into your phone as soon as you answer it. You tap the 'End Call' button.

The phone rings seconds later and you let it ring three times before answering. "Did you just fucking hang up on me?" she starts in and again you press 'End Call.'

The phone rings again and when you answer it's quiet on the other end. "Hello?" you say, like a civilized human being.

"Hello. I'm sorry," Ashley says. You can tell it's taking all of her energy to keep her voice and words under control. "You need to get over here right now."

"I need to?"

"Okay. I need you to." There's a long pause and then she says, "Please?"

That's not a word you hear her say too often which makes you think it might even be important.

"My car got totaled, so I'll have to take the bus," you tell her.

"Fuck! Take a taxi and I'll pay for it when you get here."

"Alright."

"Thank you," she says and hangs up. You wonder if you've ever heard those words out of her mouth.

Ashley lives in a lakeside home on a wooded lot on the west side of town. She's waiting for you at the door with a handful of twenties which you use to pay the taxi driver. When you return to the door Ashley hugs you tightly and you can feel her body trembling. She's the same height as you with light brown hair that's always in a braid and she's always wearing the latest fashion dress.

"What's the matter?" you ask her, holding her body snug against yours.

"I want you to kill him!" she says and begins sobbing into your shoulder.

> If you tell her "Of course," go to Scene 71.
> If you say, "That's crazy," go to Scene 72.

You pull the Range Rover to the side of the road thinking that maybe you can talk your way out of whatever the problem may be. You figure they've got to have probable cause to search the vehicle and you haven't been speeding or anything.

The two unmarked police cars stop behind you side by side and an undercover Ford Explorer comes out of nowhere and is parked in front of you. Half a dozen men swarm out of the vehicles, all of them wearing ballistic vests and pointing guns at you. The insignia on their hats and vests read: DEA.

They drag you out of the Range Rover and throw you to the ground, frisking you and cuffing you and throwing you in the back of a car. You are taken to a holding cell downtown and sit for almost two hours before you're taken to an interrogation room with two detectives who look tired and angry.

"I want my lawyer," you say to the men.

"Is that really how you want to play this?" the smaller, older detective asks. "Because we've been watching Maggot's locker for two weeks."

You keep a poker face, not trying to give a reaction to hearing Maggot's name.

"Oh, that's right," the younger Asian detective says. "We know who Maggot is and we know who you are. You're nobody."

"We don't give a fuck about you," the older man says. "You can walk today if you give us a little cooperation."

"Otherwise you're looking at a minimum of twenty years in the federal pen for the quantity of meth you had on you."

"But we know it's not yours. Maggot sent you into a trap."

"And there's only one way out," the Asian detective says.

> If you tell them the only person you're talking to is a lawyer, go to Scene 73.
> If you agree to cooperate with the detectives, go to Scene 74.

You know that nothing good could come from pulling over - you're an ex-felon with a suitcase full of drugs. You punch the gas pedal down just as another unmarked Ford Explorer comes skidding around the corner in front of you. You swerve up onto a curb and speed across a dirt lot. The three police vehicles cut through the dust behind you with lights flashing and sirens blaring.

You come out onto a road that runs parallel with the river and about a mile ahead you see a marina. The thought runs through your mind that if you can get into the water with all the dope bags open, the meth will dissolve and disappear in the river. Of course that would mean losing the six figures worth of dope which surely Maggot wouldn't be too happy about.

> If you make a move for the river, go to Scene 75.
> If you try to save the dope and keep driving, go to Scene 76.

You pluck the small pill out of her hand and toss it in your mouth. Alicia hands you a small bottle of Patron to wash it down. She cups her hand and puts it to her mouth and then grabs the Patron from you and takes a long drink. You watch the muscles of her neck work which in turns begins to get one of your muscles to work.

"Are you feeling something?" she asks.

"Oh, I'm feeling something alright," you say and look down at your crotch.

She leans into you, her half exposed breast rubbing against your arm. "You want to fuck me, don't you?" she asks.

"Oh yeah."

"Do you want to do other things to me?"

"Oh yeah."

"Like what?"

The Town Car is moving as you slip your hand through the slit in Alicia's dress and you turn her in the seat, lifting her thigh up towards the headrest. You push her dress aside and as you hoped and expected, she's not wearing any panties. You drop one of your knees to the floorboard and your head dips down to her beautiful, moist pussy that's just begging to be licked. Your tongue parts her pussy lips and your nose brushes against her clit and you remember no more.

You awaken to the sound of arguing.

"Did you like it?" you hear a loud man's voice ask.

"That's not the point," a woman's voice replies. "I had to do something until the pill kicked in."

You open your eyes to see Maggot and Alicia standing beside you.

"So, you were going to fuck my wife, huh?" Maggot says to you.

> Go to Scene 77.

It seems to go against almost every fiber of your being but you turn the pill down. Alicia puffs out her bottom lip and says, "What, you don't want to fuck me?"

You look at her and say, "You're one of the most beautiful women I've seen. If you weren't Maggot's girl I'd fuck you like you've never been fucked before."

"Oh really," she says, arching her eyebrows.

"Without a doubt," you promise her. "But I can't fuck around with you if I'm having dealings with your man. That's a good way for someone to get killed."

As the Town Car rolls to a stop Alicia says, "Damn, and I wasn't even wearing any panties."

You look at the long slit in her dress showing all leg and say, "That's what I was afraid of."

The back door opens and you see it's Maggot. He helps Alicia out of the car. "You win, darling," she tells him. "He's loyal."

Maggot laughs. "I knew it!"

"What the fuck's going on?" you ask as you get out of the car and find yourself in a large warehouse.

"Relax," Maggot says, "it was just a little test. And you passed with flying colors. Alicia was pretty certain she'd get you with these," Maggot says and gives her breast a squeeze.

Maggot throws an arm around your shoulder and leads you to a doorway in the warehouse. "I need someone like you I can trust. Work with me and you can have anything you want." He puts a hand on the door knob.

> If you say you'll work with Maggot, go to Scene 78.
> If you decline his offer, go to Scene 51.

The next evening you borrow a friend's car with the promise that you will bring him back some meth. You drive out to the suburbs and slowly drive past Maggot's house twice - it looks dark and empty. You park a couple of blocks away and walk casually to Maggot's house. When you're pretty sure nobody is looking you sneak into the backyard.

There's a sliding glass door on a deck that leads to the kitchen and dining area, and another sliding glass door at the basement level. Both are locked and are secured with two-by-fours in their tracks to prevent jimmying. You check all of the windows that you can reach but all are securely locked. There's a wooden door at the side of the house that leads to the garage and is secured with a deadbolt.

Thirty seconds later, with the aid of a small crowbar you brought along, you're through the door. Inside the garage is another door which leads into the house which is secured with another locked deadbolt which you proceed to destroy with the crowbar. The fact that Maggot is this security conscious has you a little concerned, and rightly so. When you get inside and look around you find nothing of any great value. What you do find is a large six foot tall gun safe secured to the floor in an office closet, and of course it's locked.

You're not sure if your luck just got better or worse as you see headlights pull into the driveway. You peek out a window and see Alicia exiting a black Town Car and walking up to the front door.

> If you sneak out the garage door and escape, go to Scene 79.
> If you decide to jump Alicia and make her open the safe, go to
  Scene 80.

Something in your gut tells you it's probably best to leave Maggot and all his dealings alone. You've learned to trust that gut instinct because when you don't you usually seem to find yourself in trouble.

You're sick and tired of being in trouble and sick and tired of being sick and tired. You've been living a pretty crazy life and have had some pretty wild times, but of course there's the downside to your lifestyle which has meant a number of years behind bars.

As you lie in bed at home and contemplate your life, you're not sure you're ready to walk the straight and narrow, but you know it wouldn't hurt to at least have a little stability.

The next morning you decide to see about getting a job.

> Go to Scene 4.

You tell Lil Taco maybe some other time and head home. On the way home you think about your job and how it's hard work but not that bad. Not to mention you can eat all the candy that you want. After your training-in period you'll get to drive your own van and it will be almost like being your own boss.

Once you arrive home you throw a frozen TV dinner into the microwave and then sit down in front of the TV to watch some mindless entertainment like the majority of American society.

Just like in prison, you get into a regular routine as the days and weeks slip quickly by. But at least you're free...or so you tell yourself. Eagerly you await the next season of "Real Housewives."

THE END

"You wanna fuck her?" Lil Taco asks you.

He's driving his purple Impala and has his seat leaned so far back that you wonder how he can even see over the steering wheel. His question catches you off guard and he laughs. "Man, I saw the way you was lookin' at her. You practically had to pick your eyeballs off the ground."

"I didn't mean any disrespect," you say from the passenger seat. "I didn't know she was your girl."

"She's one of my girls," Lil Taco says. "Ain't that right, Rosa?"

"I better be your number one," she says from the back seat. You glance over your shoulder to find that she's removed her red and white work shirt and is wearing only a white frilly bra. She's chewing bubble gum and playing with her phone.

"Of course you is, baby," he says to her. He smiles at you and says, "So, you wanna fuck her?"

"What, I don't get a say in the matter?" Rosa asks.

"What is there to say? You tellin' me you won't fuck my man?"

"I don't know," she says and pops a pink bubble. "Does he have a big dick?"

"How do I know what dick he's got?" He looks at you and asks, "Do you have a big dick?"

"It gets the job done," you say.

"I can tell you he has big balls if even half the stories are true of some of the shit him and Roberto were into."

"Aw, I miss Roberto," she says with another pop of a bubble. Lil Taco does the sign of the cross with his right hand over his chest. Rosa puts a hand on your shoulder and says, "Alright, let's fuck."

> If you go along with fucking Rosa, go to Scene 81.
> If you tell Rosa maybe some other time, go to Scene 82.

Blinky's is a small hole in the wall bar with a long bar along one wall and ten high back booths along the other wall with barely enough room to walk between them, especially when the place is packed like it is on this night. You bump and push your way toward the back booth and LT walks sideways but his bulk still jars everybody he walks by.

Sitting at the last booth is a muscular Latino with close cropped black hair and goatee. He has a white gold chain around his neck, a matching bracelet, and a couple thick white gold rings with diamonds in them. When he sees you he smiles and you imagine it's what a snake looks like when it smiles.

"My man," Ramone says to you and puts out his hand. You slap his wrist away.

"Where's my eight grand?" you ask him.

"It's in the works," he answers and then adds, "Wait, what? It's six grand."

"Interest, motherfucker. You were supposed to have my money over two weeks ago. Now where is it?"

"I tell you, man, I got a big deal going down. Tonight, dawg. I'll have your money next week, sure thing."

You look at LT standing beside you with his big arms crossed and then back at Ramone. "You make no sense. You tell me you don't have my money but you've got a deal tonight? How do you have a deal without money?"

"It's complicated," Ramone says. "Just give me until next week and I'll drop ten stacks on you, guaranteed."

> If you agree to getting paid next week, go to Scene 83.
> If you yank Ramone out of the booth and drag him to the bathroom, go to Scene 84.

Sitting in the Suburban a block away you and LT watch the front door of Blinky's. There are quite a few people in and out of the bar and it's almost half an hour before you see Ramone leave the bar. He's a short Latino with prison muscles and a lot of white gold jewelry. Walking beside him is a tough looking black guy with two more black guys walking behind them.

"The guy walking with Ramone is Top Floor," LT says.

"Top Floor?" you ask.

"Yeah, he likes to throw people from the top floors of buildings. All three of those guys are part of DSK." You look at LT with the expression of who the fuck are they. "Death Squad Killas. A south side gang that requires a murder to join."

"They look like punks."

"And any punk can pull a trigger."

"What the fuck is Ramone doing with them?" you ponder out loud.

"One way to find out," LT says as he starts the SUV.

You watch as Ramone and Top Floor get in a nondescript Dodge minivan, which leaves the bar followed by a silver Dodge Charger with the other two DSK members. LT follows from a distance until you all end up at an abandoned construction site on the outskirts of the city. LT stops and parks in the shadows a couple blocks away.

"Do you have any firepower?" you ask LT.

He pushes a couple buttons on the center console to reveal a secret compartment under the dashboard that has two large pistols.

> If you approach the construction site to see what's going on, go to Scene 85.

> If you decide to wait and watch the vehicles, go to Scene 86.

The Rottweiler is jumping and barking as it follows you step for step on the other side of the fence. You finally cross the street and look over your shoulder at the menacing dog you leave behind. From the glow of the street lamp on the corner you see that you're leaving quite a trail of blood behind you.

Your injuries are excruciating and you figure it's only by the power of adrenaline that you're able to keep moving. You're pretty sure there's a river or pond or something a couple blocks away and you decide to go there to clean up so the cops can't find you by merely following your blood trail.

You cut through an alley and the leg the dog chomped on gives out on you. You fall to the grimy concrete and use your good arm and all of your strength to drag yourself behind a Dumpster and out of plain view. You can't believe how cold you feel but you're too weak and tired to do anything except bleed. You close your eyes and they never open again.

THE END

You start up the van and drive it up to the warehouse garage door. You hop out and jog to the wall and press the 'Open' button. As soon as the garage door starts to lift a loud alarm starts to blare. You jump even though you're anticipating this. What you weren't anticipating was seeing the Rottweiler attack dog growling under the garage door as soon as there was space enough for him to fit his head. He must have jumped on and rattled the gate enough to knock the chain loose.

The large dog's nails are clicking on the pavement as he pulls himself into the warehouse, his growl filling the empty building. You run for the van and hear the dog barking and running right behind you. You don't dare look over your shoulder because it makes no difference - either you'll make it to the van or you won't.

You grab the door of the van and swing yourself into the driver's seat. The dog rams the door with his body, slamming it shut loudly behind you. The dog jumps at your face, teeth bared, but only gets saliva and froth all over the window.

"Fuck you!" you say and give the dog the finger as you drive out of the warehouse. The dog runs alongside of the van for half a block before stopping and turning back to its domain.

After a couple of blocks you turn onto another street and no longer hear the alarm in the distance. There's still work to do - unloading the money, ditching the van, lugging sacks full of change to machines across the city to convert it all to paper money - but you're happy with the night's haul. You make more in one night than you would have working at that place for six months. You give yourself a little pat on the back.

THE END

After taking a little breather, you decide it would be stupid to leave any of the money behind seeing as you're already here. You spend the next two hours loading up every last box of rolled nickels and pennies until your arms are aching so much you can hardly lift them. You're drenched in sweat and breathing like an eighty-year-old asthmatic. As you get in the van you notice through a warehouse skylight that it's already getting light outside.

You start the vehicle, put it in 'Drive' and as it starts to move you hear a terrible grinding noise. You hop out and notice that the load in the van is so heavy that the wheel wells are rubbing against the back wheels. There's no way you can drive like this.

"Sonofabitch!" you say as you swing open the back doors of the van and begin toppling out all of the boxes of pennies. Thankfully those were the last that you loaded. Heavy boxes crash to the floor, penny rolls breaking open and scattering everywhere. After almost twenty minutes of frantic work you freeze when you hear a sound: it's the warehouse garage door opening up.

"Shit!" You run to the driver's seat and punch the gas as the large door rises. Boxes of coins tumble out the back as you forgot to secure the rear doors of the van. But it makes little difference as the front of the van crashes into the grilles of two police cars parked in front of the warehouse.

You're dragged out of the van, too tired to run or resist. As you sit in jail you have plenty of time to think about how you screwed up and how you'll do it differently next time.

THE END

The .44 Magnum bucks in your hand and the explosion of the discharging shell is deafening in the small jewelry store. The heavy slug hits the man in the back shoulder and propels him off his feet and through the glass door. The man lands on the sidewalk in a thousand sparkling shards of broken glass and a growing red pool of blood.

All three of the ladies in the jewelry store scream but their voices are quickly drowned out by a blaring alarm ringing in the store.

Tony comes running out of the back with a gym bag full of loot and says to you, "I thought there was no alarm!"

"I said there was no silent alarm," you reply.

"C'mon, let's go!" Tony says and you race to the door, not having to open it since it was shattered by the body. A police car races across the parking lot toward you and Tony as you run to your getaway car. Both of you open up with gunfire on the cop, riddling the car with bullet holes until it slams into a parked car.

Your getaway car is a newer Cadillac that Tony jacked from a car wash earlier in the day. "Holy shit, we're having fun now!" he hollers as he guns the car out of the parking lot.

"The verdict's out on that," you say. "No fun if we get caught."

"Oh fuck," your partner says and you see what he sees: two police cars with lights flashing and sirens blaring, coming right at you less than a hundred yards away.

Tony slides the car around the next corner and moments later the police cars follow suit.

> Go to Scene 87.

You let the customer go knowing that gunfire would likely raise even more alarms and attention.

"We've got to go!" you yell in a low voice. A moment later Tony appears at your side with a gym bag like yours full of loot from the safe. You rush out the front doors of The Golden Scepter and you see the customer who escaped waving down a police car twenty yards away.

"What the fuck!?" Tony exclaims as the two of you run toward the newer Cadillac that is your getaway car.

An alarm starts blaring from the jewelry store and the cop car hits its lights and siren and gives chase as Tony steers the car out of the parking lot. Within moments there are two more cop cars on your tail.

> Go to Scene 87.

"No way, I'm not going to do that," Noelle says to you.

"It's your first time, I want you to be safe," you tell her.

"If I wanted safe I wouldn't be doing a robbery with you. I'm not sitting in the car playing getaway driver. I want to be in on the action with you."

"Are you crazy?" you ask her seriously.

"Obviously," she replies just as serious.

You smile and kiss her deeply, your hands squeezing her tight ass.

At 9:30 on a Monday morning you and Noelle approach the side door of an eighteen theater Cineplex that you've scoped out a couple of times before. You're both wearing clear plastic masks that distort your features but from a distance are unnoticeable. Noelle has on a dark colored wig and you're wearing a stocking cap that hides your hair.

The door is propped open by a baseball sized rock and once inside you both pull out pistols and move quickly to the office where you find the overweight manager stuffing his face with donuts.

"Open the safe," you tell the shocked man with jelly filling on his nose. He tries to say something but only unintelligible crumbs fall out of his mouth.

"Do it now!" Noelle yells and presses the barrel of her pistol against his forehead.

Trembling, the crotch of his pants soaked in urine, the manager falls to his knees and crawls to the safe. When the door opens you toss him a backpack and tell him to fill it up.

Noelle stands beside you, her gun pointed at the back of the manager's head, her body trembling with excitement. She grabs your free hand and sticks it under her skirt where you feel her soaking wet pantyless pussy.

> Go to Scene 88.

Rather than push your luck, you take Noelle to Cancun where there's a lot of different types of pushing happening: pushing her from behind, pushing on top of her, pushing her on top of you. It's sun and fun all day, dancing all night and nonstop fucking in between all those times. Sometimes it feels damn good to be a criminal.

And whether or not you perpetrate any other crimes with Noelle is still to be seen, but you know it's a dangerous path to tread putting your safety and trust in another's hands. As good as it feels right now to have this beautiful woman on your team, you're smart enough to know that most relationships never last forever and if a criminal relationship ends bad, it ends very bad.

But for now, life is good as you watch Noelle step dripping wet out of the shower and she walks toward you sitting on the bed.

THE END

The tires of the Escalade squeal around the corner and Rocco zigzags through traffic but the cop car stays on your tail. Cars waiting at a red light block the intersection ahead and the Escalade veers onto a sidewalk and enters a large park, bouncing across the grass. People lounging, playing Frisbee, joggers, all dive out of the way as the large SUV races by, followed now by two police cars with their lights and sirens on blast.

You, Chaz and the teller bounce wildly in the back seat and then you're being squished against the door with the teller and Chaz pressed against you as the Escalade slides sideways down a steep embankment. You feel and hear the crunch of metal against metal as one of the cop cars rams into the rear side panel of the SUV.

The teller screams as the truck begins to roll and the three of you in the backseat tumble around like clothes in a dryer machine. All of the side windows of the SUV shatter as the vehicle does one and half rolls landing on its roof in a small ravine.

As you crawl out of the wrecked vehicle you see the two cop cars parked at the top of the hill and four police officers with guns drawn running towards you. You look towards Chaz who's trying to pull the teller out through a side window and Rocco is still trying to get his seatbelt undone.

"Get your hands up! Put your hands up now! Don't move!" the police are yelling.

Yeah, that's not going to happen, you think to yourself. You've already killed one cop, there's no going back now. You bring your gun up and begin firing. You see a couple of the cops go down, but whether due to your bullets or to seek cover, you don't know. At least three bullets are stopped by your body armor, but one round strikes you in the face and you don't know anything ever again.

THE END

"As soon as you take the next corner, let's jump out and scatter before they have a chance to get more backup," you say.

"You're taking the money?" Chaz asks.

"You've got the hostage," you tell him. "Do you want to trade?"

"No, I trust you. We'll meet up at Shaggy's tonight at eight."

Rocco turns onto a residential street and parks the Escalade at an angle in the middle of the street. Chaz fires off a couple of rounds through the side window at the cop car which slams on its brakes and stops sideways twenty feet away.

All of you slide out of the SUV on the opposite side from the cop car. Rocco fires a couple of rounds over the hood of the truck to keep the cop's heads down. More sirens can be heard from various points off in the distance.

You bolt between some cars, across a lawn and then in between a couple of houses. You look over your shoulder and see Chaz dragging his hostage across the other side of the street and disappearing between houses. You hear gunfire as Rocco ducks and weaves his way down to the end of the street and around the corner.

Running down an alley you see a cop car drive past and then hear the screeching of brakes. You quickly jump a fence, go through some yards and then run across another street.

You catch a guy about to get into his car and jack him for his ride. Five minutes later you're out of the area that is soon swarming with cops.

> If you meet up with Chaz to split the money, go to Scene 89.
> If you decide to keep all of the money for yourself, go to Scene 90.

You know there's no way the big SUV is going to outrun the cop car and certainly not the cop radio, and the longer you wait the more there are going to be. You look at Chaz and say, "Let's take the motherfuckers out."

"Next corner, hit the brakes," Chaz tells Rocco and he does.

You and Chaz throw open the back doors as the cop car comes to a screeching halt ten yards behind the Escalade. The .357 rocks in your hand as you fire rounds into the windshield of the cop car and the two officers inside it. You hear the full auto rattle of Chaz's Tec-9 and the bullets piercing metal and glass.

The cop's rear tires spin and produce white smoke as the vehicle begins to back up. You both continue firing into the car and you can see blood splattered on the inside of the shattered windshield. The cop car rams backwards into two parked cars and stops moving and no one gets out.

You and Chaz jump back in the Escalade and Rocco takes off.

"How far to the switch car?" you ask.

"Just a few blocks," Rocco says.

"What about her?" you ask, referring to the trembling teller next to you.

"Honey, do you want to join Trump's team?" Chaz asks her.

She shakes her head and Chaz laughs, "I don't blame you." He duct tapes her hands, feet and a strip across her eyes and leaves her in the stolen Escalade as the three of you get into a blue and white taxi cab. While Rocco drives you and Chaz count the money in the back seat and split three ways you each walk away with nearly thirty-five grand.

"Let's do it again sometime," Chaz says as he drops you off near your place. You nod your head and give him a thumbs up.

THE END

Lloyd turns out to be a tall, muscular guy in his twenties who looks like a typical gym rat that's probably injecting steroids. No doubt your ex is fucking him any chance she gets.

He works for a courier company called Zippy's and you follow him on his route in a rented Nissan Altima. The grey car is unnoticeable. Seeing as you know the insured package is in the white van he drives, you'd like to just jack him for the whole vehicle at his next stop but Gina made you promise you wouldn't rob him. You agreed, not because you cared about Gina's feelings but because of the chance that if he were robbed it might be seen as an inside job and linked back to Gina and then you.

So you have no choice but to wait until delivery is made and to then figure out your next move. You follow the van at a distance into the projects but the house he stops at is well kept with a fenced in lawn and well tended shrubs and flowers around the house. There's a 'Beware of Dog' sign on the porch and near the front steps a sign with an alarm company's name and logo.

You watch Lloyd walk up to the front door from your car a block away. He carries a small white box that looks like about the size of a paperback book. You can't imagine how that could be worth six figures and wonder if Gina's info is bullshit. But the house does stand out and piques your interest. Lloyd drives off and you sit watching the house.

A young black kid pushes a bike with a flat tire down the middle of the street and you ask him if he knows who lives in that house.

"Fuck you, cop," the little kid says as he keeps walking.

> If you decide to impersonate a cop and approach the house, go to Scene 91.
> If you decide to keep staking out the home, go to Scene 92.

Hot water sprays from the showerhead onto you and Gina. You have her face and big tits pressed up against the clear sliding shower door as you vigorously fuck her from behind. You twirl your hand around her dark, wet hair and pull her head back to you so you can stick your tongue in her mouth which she sucks on greedily.

The thrusting of your hips increases, your wet bodies slapping together faster and harder. You slide your hands down her wet hips and you grasp her tightly as you pound into her spasming pussy. She screams out in ecstasy and begs you not to stop.

You fuck her faster and harder than you ever have as your cock leads you into a state of nirvana and you try to hold it for as long as you can then you're exploding like a Yellowstone geyser and grunting like a grizzly bear. The next thing you know the two of you are falling out of the shower as the sliding door pops out of its track and crashes to the floor.

"Holy fuck that was amazing," Gina says after she catches her breath.

"Yeah, we do still have that, don't we?" you say as you get up and get a towel.

"So are you going to check out the score I told you about?" she asks.

You shake your head. "It's not good to mix business and pleasure. Besides, I don't work with people I don't trust."

She looks hurt as you walk out of the bathroom to get dressed.

"Hey, what about my shower door?"

"Have Lloyd fix it," you say.

"Fuck you!"

"Yep, another time," you answer.

> Go to Scene 28.

"How have I not met you before this?" you ask Beth as the two of you sit in the back booth of a twenty four hour restaurant. You're amazed at how much the two of you have in common and both with the same type of humor.

"I just got here from Colorado," she says. "I'm a friend of Kelly's."

"I don't know Kelly but I know Colorado has some killer weed."

"You like to smoke?" she asks.

"I do. But I like to make money more," you say with a smile.

"Me too," she answers with the same smile.

"Is that why you're here, to make money?"

She nods her head.

"How's that working for you?" you ask.

"Well, Kelly's connect seems kind of flaky, so I'm not really sure yet." She stares at you a few moments as she tries to work something out in her head. Then she asks you, "Do you know a lot of people around here?"

"Oh yeah, been in the area all my life."

"How much green do you think you could move?" Beth asks you.

"How much do you got?"

She smiles and takes you to a farm house half an hour out of the city. You follow her into a barn where there's a moving truck. She opens the back and you see furniture and boxes.

"Gotta make it look real," she says. "Help me get this stuff out."

You toss it all to the side and then she reveals boxes of triple sealed vacuum packed packages of top grade marijuana. "Fifty pounds worth," she says.

> If you decide to jack her for her weed, go to Scene 93.
> If you help her move the product, go to Scene 94.

"Would you like to come in?" you ask Beth as she pulls up to your place.

She accompanies you inside where you put on some music and pour a couple of drinks. "You don't need to get me drunk to take advantage of me," she says with a smile.

You set the drinks aside and push her back against the wall as you kiss her. She eagerly accepts your tongue and then clasps both her hands to your ass cheeks. You moan in pleasant surprise as you continue kissing her and slide a hand up under her sweater. You slip your fingers inside her bra cup and pinch her nipple causing her to shudder.

In a flurry of motion pants are coming down, shirts are coming off, panties and boxers and bra are falling to the floor and you're pulling her to your bedroom. You lay her on her back on your comfy bed and you nuzzle your face into her succulent pussy, licking and sucking until she's crying out in delight. She twists her body around so you're in the sixty nine position and she begins sucking and stroking your hard cock as you continue to lick and finger her excited pussy.

You reposition yourself as you rise up on your knees and push her onto her back. You slip your throbbing cock between her legs and then grab her hips and pull her into you, your cock pushing all the way into her.

"Oh yes," she gasps, "oh yes," as your hips jerk frantically back and forth. Her hands reach to your face and she pulls you down to her so she can kiss you as you continue fucking her, her tits rubbing back and forth against your chest.

Her body shivers and shakes like an earthquake as your cock explodes and fills her with your warmth. After another session an hour or so later she gets dressed and leaves on wobbly legs. You put your hands behind your head and look at the ceiling and figure it hasn't been too bad of a day.

THE END

You carry Molly out to the van, no one in the tattoo shop giving you a second glance as you carry the woman wearing only bra and panties over your shoulder. Once in the back of the van you lay her on the bed and then pull the tape from her mouth. She doesn't even cry out but instead says, "Please don't take me to him. He's going to kill me, I know it. Please, you've got to help me."

"What did you do this time?" you ask Molly. It seems she and Will are always on some strange drama bullshit that you can never understand.

"I didn't do anything," she says. "Really. I mean I slept with those two guys but I did it for Will, to get him some information."

"What did you get?"

"Gonorrhea, but I got some pills for that."

You shake your head. "No, what information did you get?"

"Oh, that. There's a guy arriving at the airport tonight with a briefcase of diamonds, like a half a mill worth."

"And these guys you fucked just gave you the info out of the blue?"

"I have my ways," she says. "Do you want to see?"

"No, you just keep taking your pills."

"You've got to help me," she pleads. "Take me to the airport and help me get those diamonds so Will can see I wasn't fucking around on him for no reason."

She sees you thinking it over and says, "Come on, please? You'll get a cut of the action as well."

> If you agree to help her, go to Scene 95.
> If you bring her back to your cousin as instructed, go to Scene 96.

You don't know what it is but you find that you can almost never say no to Ashley. Because she comes from money - her dad's a big shot CEO and her mom owns boutique clothing stores on each coast - you figure it's good to keep her in your corner, but it's also something more than that which you can't quite explain. You two have fucked a few times, though not since she's been with her new guy Roger, but the sex is never that great because she's so damn self centered - it's all about her. Nonetheless you care about her and want to see her happy.

"Is it Roger?" you ask after she's stopped crying.

"No," she says incredulously. "Why would I want Roger dead?"

"I don't know. After a few months you're always about ready to kill whatever guy you're with."

"We've only been dating two months," she says indignantly. "No, I want you to kill Brandon."

"Who the fuck is Brandon?"

"He's a minister that's been screwing my mother and he's about to file a lawsuit against my father. If he succeeds I'll lose millions of dollars in my inheritance."

"You want me to kill a minister?"

"I'll give you whatever you want. But it has to be tonight because I found out he's filing the paperwork tomorrow. He'll be at his church until ten or you can catch him at home - I have the address for both."

"I'll need a gun and a car," you tell her.

"Take Roger's Porsche," she says and hands you the keys. "He has a gun in the glove box. Thank you, baby, you're the best."

> If you drive to the church, go to Scene 97.
> If you drive to the home, go to Scene 99.

"Calm down, baby, tell me what's going on," you say to Ashley. She can't stop crying and you feel your shoulder becoming wet beneath your shirt from her tears. She says something about her family being torn apart and her future ruined and millions of dollars but none of it is making any sense to you.

Regardless of it making sense or not, you have no intention of killing anyone for Ashley. Not because you have anything against killing someone but because you don't like the thought of giving Ashley, or anyone for that matter, that kind of power over you. As soon as you kill for someone else they can always hold that over your head and use it against you to make you do pretty much whatever they want.

"Please," Ashley begs, "I'll do anything if you do this for me."

You raise your eyebrows and look at her. "Anything?"

"Well I won't cheat on my boyfriend but I can give you a blowjob if you want."

"I don't think there's ever been a time I didn't want a blowjob," you say.

No sooner are the words out of your mouth that she has your zipper down, your cock out and in her mouth. You're not hard but her warm, moist sucking has you growing in her hot mouth. She sucks you like her favorite lollipop, reaching her fingers into your zipper and pulling out your balls that she plays with while bobbing on your knob until you're gushing into her mouth.

"So you'll do it?" she asks as she wipes her mouth.

"I didn't say that."

"You asshole," she says and begins crying.

> If you tell her you're kidding, that you'll do it, go to Scene 71.
> If you turn and leave, go to Scene 99.

You lawyer up and don't say a word to the detectives because you've never snitched in your life and not about to do so now. Doing the right thing you thought for sure Maggot would come through and help you with an attorney. When he doesn't come through you're stuck with a public defender and the best deal he's able to work out for you is 100 months in the federal prison system. That means you'll be serving 85 months minimum, a little over seven years.

Not once does that maggot Maggot put any money on your books and you think about what you're going to do to him once you get out. But that's going to be awhile.

THE END

You convince yourself that it's not really snitching seeing as the cops already know whose dope it is. And you sure as hell don't intend to go serve no twenty years for some guy you barely know and who, it seems, pretty much sent you into a trap.

You tell the detectives what you know, which you don't think is really much, and for your cooperation you only have to serve a 60 month sentence in the federal prison system. Your statement helps the DEA convict Maggot to almost 188 months.

Because you go into the joint with a snitch jacket, you find yourself in protective custody units doing hard time. Yet before even your first year is up you find yourself stuck fourteen times in the back and neck from a prison shiv and you bleed out before they can get you to the hospital.

THE END

You reach the marina and slam the Range Rover through a locked gate. The three unmarked cop vehicles are right on your ass with their lights flashing and sirens blaring. There's no way you'd make it to the river if you jumped out of your SUV with the suitcase of meth.

Time for Plan B, you say to yourself as you gun the engine and race past the rows of docked boats. You pull the small suitcase into your lap and put the windows down on the truck. Once you're past the boats the pavement raises a few feet above the water level and it comes to an end fifteen yards ahead of you with a marshy bog beyond. The cops surely figure they've got you cornered.

You jerk the steering wheel and the Range Rover goes airborne as it leaves the pavement and flies into the river, hitting the water with a jarring splash. Immediately you begin tearing into the bags of meth and letting it all loose into the river as the SUV begins to drift in the river's flow and then starts to sink. When your task is finished you swim to the edge of the river where you're promptly arrested.

They have no evidence to hold you and you're released a few hours later. When you finally make it to Maggot's, he's already heard the news.

"You lost my truck and my drugs," he says to you.

"Fuck you, Maggot! You sent me into a trap and you know it. I want the ten grand you owe me."

"You didn't keep your end of the agreement," Maggot says. "But I do like how fast you think on your feet. I'll tell you what, if you take care of something for me I'll pay you twenty grand and we'll be square. Deal?"

> If you take his offer, go to Scene 78.
> If you tell him to go fuck himself, go to Scene 100.

You race past the marina with the cops hot on your tail. You know you're not going to ditch the cops on the streets; you need to get off road in some woods or something and utilize the Range Rover's four wheel drive. About a mile ahead there's a bridge that goes over the river and you're pretty sure there are some rocky hills on the other side you can lose your pursuers in.

A marked local cop car and a county sheriff's vehicle join the chase as you reach the bridge. Halfway across the river you see the roadblock. You gun the engine and go for it. Ten yards in front of the roadblock you run over two strips of StopStiks that flatten three of the SUV's tires. Cops dive out of the way as you ram through the roadblock and you duck down as you hear handguns and shotguns firing, their slugs piercing the front and sides of the truck.

You feel a burning pain in your side and another in your arm and you're not happy when you look down to see blood. The Range Rover is struck from behind from a pursuing cop car and the SUV spins out of control, orange and white sparks flying up from the three bare rims.

Before you know it, the side window is smashed and you're being yanked out the opening and thrown hard to the road and cuffed.

You're taken to a locked unit at the hospital and after surgery you're visited by two detectives.

"We know the drugs belong to Maggot," one of the detectives says.

"We don't give a shit about you," the other detective pipes in. "You give us Maggot and you can walk."

"Otherwise you're looking at twenty years federal time. It's your choice."

> If you tell them to go fuck themselves, go to Scene 73.
> If you decide to cooperate, go to Scene 74.

You're lying on a dirty concrete floor in a large warehouse. You try to sit up but you realize your hands are cuffed behind you and you're still woozy from whatever the pill was that you took. Your gut explodes with pain as Maggot's booted foot kicks you.

"I asked you a question, asshole," he says to you.

"She came onto me," you groan in pain.

"Of course she did, you stupid fuck. It was a test to see where your loyalty lies. I can't trust you with my woman which means I certainly can't trust you with my business."

"I wasn't going to fuck her," you say.

"Then you're even stupider than I thought because she's an amazing fuck."

"He's a liar, too," Alicia says standing next to her man. "He would have done anything I let him do, or told him to do."

"Bullshit," you say.

Alicia sticks out her foot towards your face, her leg poking through her dress slit and showing skin all the way to her hip. "Lick my shoe," she says.

You tell her to go fuck herself.

Another kick from Maggot curls you up into a fetal position.

"Fuck you, too," you moan.

"Wrong answer," Maggot says and you clinch up in anticipation of another kick. Instead you see him and Alicia walking away and Maggot stops and addresses the Town Car driver that you notice for the first time. "Take care of that trash," Maggot says before he and his wife leave.

The last thing you remember is seeing the big driver walking towards you with a heavy pipe in his hand. You wake up three weeks later in ICU wearing a full body cast.

THE END

The fact that Maggot and Alicia put you to the test makes you respect their game a little more. Obviously they run a tight ship and you're curious as to what Maggot's main operation is. Maybe it can be the stepping stone you need to get yourself up and running. You agree to work with him.

He opens the door inside the warehouse and brings you into a large room filled with dozens of wooden crates. All of the crates have foreign writing on them, Russian you think. Maggot pops open one of the crates to show you half a dozen assault rifles. Another crate contains hand grenades. Others are filled with various weapons from machine pistols to sniper rifles.

"All of these items are set up for delivery in three days," Maggot tells you. "I've got a driver and my right hand man Leroy to take care of the money transaction. What I need you to do is ride shotgun and make sure the deal goes smoothly."

Three days later you're riding in a delivery truck that has pretzel advertisings on the sides, the rear filled with weaponry. The driver, Stan, parks behind a grocery store in the northern suburbs. Shortly after you arrive an older model white Suburban arrives and three guys step out.

"How are they going to fit the crates in that?" you ask.

"If the money's all there, we just swap vehicles with them," Leroy says.

As you get out of the truck you notice that everyone is armed and the tension is high, everyone watching everyone.

"Where's the cash?" Leroy asks the man standing in the middle of the trio.

"Let's see the merchandise first," he responds.

> Go to Scene 101.

You hate the thought of leaving the scene of a burglary without any loot to show for it, but you're not too keen being caught inside someone else's home, especially when you're practically unarmed. You sneak off out the back and get the hell out of the neighborhood.

You return your friend's car and he's pissed you came back empty handed. You tell him shit fell through and that you'll look out for him another time. You toss him his keys and walk away.

> Go to Scene 28.

You hide behind the wall that divides the kitchen from the living room, kicking yourself that you didn't bring a mask or a weapon. You grab a large kitchen knife from the butcher's block upon the counter.

The front door opens and then closes and you press your back against the wall as you wait for the lights to be turned on. They remain off and you hear the clicking of Alicia's heels as she walks away from your position and down a hallway that leads to the bedroom.

As you sneak down the hallway, you see the light coming from the bedroom and you can hear Alicia humming to herself. You take a deep breath, ready yourself, and rush into the bedroom. It's empty.

You hear the water to the bathtub being turned on in the adjoining bathroom. As you creep up to the door you see Alicia standing with her back to you in front of the tub. The dress she's wearing, a sexy gold evening gown, falls to the floor and your eyes are drawn to her nakedness, especially her heart shaped ass.

You almost feel bad for doing this, but it's too late to back out now. You rush her and throw your arm around her throat. She screams and struggles but you let her see the knife and she calms down.

"I'm not going to hurt you," you growl in her ear, trying to make your voice sound different lest she recognize you. "I just want you to open the safe."

"Only my husband has the combination," she whimpers.

> If you tie her up and wait for Maggot, go to Scene 102.
> If you decide to tie her up and have a little fun with her, go to Scene 103.
> If you tie her up and leave, go to Scene 79.

As you suspected, when Rosa peels off her tight, yellow pants you see she's wearing nothing underneath. She has a sweet little pussy with an upside down triangle of groomed fur above her slit. She undoes her bra and her perky breasts curve like ski jumps. Your cock has sprung to life and is straining against the fabric of your pants.

"Do you need help?" she asks and then pops her bubble gum.

You quickly disrobe and she seems pleased with what she sees. Rosa wraps a hand around your hard cock and leads you to the shower, which you're thankful for after a hard day in the warehouse. She does a wonderful job of soaping your body, spending extra time on your cock, balls and ass. Suddenly you feel one of her slippery, soapy digits poking into your asshole.

"Whoa!" you say and pull her hand away.

"Some guys like that," she tells you.

"And some guys like to fuck farm animals. I don't judge, but I'm not one of those guys."

"What kind of guy are you then?"

You take her to the bedroom and show her, fucking her six ways from Sunday until she's screaming and moaning and you finish off straddling her torso as you titty fuck her and give her a pearl necklace.

After an hour of fun you meet up with Lil Taco and he offers you a business proposition.

> If you accept his proposal, go to Scene 104.
> If you tell him you've got to work in the morning, go to Scene 52.

"I appreciate the offer," you say, "but no thanks."

Rosa squeezes your shoulder. "Oh, I understand. You're gay? That's cool, I know a lot of guys who like to suck dick. I learned some good tricks from one."

"Is true, Holmes," Lil Taco says. "She does this thing with her tongue--"

"I'm not gay," you tell them.

"Ohhhh," Rosa says and looks over your shoulder and into your lap. "You're embarrassed because you have a little peepee?"

"My peepee is plenty big," you state.

"So what's the problem?" Lil Taco asks.

"This is just strange," you say. "I guess I've never had some guy trying to get me to fuck his girl. It almost feels like a trap."

"I don't have the clap," Rosa says.

Lil Taco laughs and says, "No, fool, she ain't my girl. She's one of my girls. I run a little business on the side. You know everyone has to have a hustle. Rosa's one of my best working girls, ain't you, Chica?"

"You know it," she says and pops her bubble gum.

"Well again, I appreciate the offer," you begin to say.

"I'm offering you a gift," Lil Taco says. "You gonna disrespect me by turning down my gift?"

> If you accept his gift and fuck Rosa, go to Scene 81.
> If you tell Lil Taco you've got to head home, go to Scene 52.

Next week comes and goes and there's no sign of Ramone. You put out the word once again that you're looking for him but no one seems to have seen or heard from him since the night you last saw him in Blinky's.

You kick yourself for letting him slide and for not being more proactive when the opportunity presented itself. Maybe that's been your problem your whole life, always waiting, not taking action when you should. You realize you've been living life like a rudderless ship, always being tossed to and fro by the waves of life like you have no say in the matter, no control.

Well you're sick of it, sick of everyone taking advantage of you, sick of constantly being fucked over by the system, sick of always feeling like the victim.

For once in your life you decide you're going to take a stand. The stand you take is atop a kitchen chair with a noose wrapped around your neck and tied to the rafter above you. You show the world that it can't pick on you any more as you kick the chair out from beneath you.

THE END

"Come on, man, what the fuck?" Ramone protests as you push him through the bathroom door. Two men are at the urinal trough and quickly zip up and leave after LT tells them the bathroom is closed.

Ramone makes a move and swings a fist at you, which is exactly what you were waiting for. You duck and hit him hard twice in the side and as he brings his arms down to shield himself you hit him with an uppercut to the jaw. Ramone crashes through a toilet stall door and lands on the piss splattered linoleum floor next to a clogged toilet that looks and smells like it's had a couple of sitters on it.

"Damn that felt good!" you say as you shake your hand. "Now give me my money."

"I told you--" he begins but flinches when you move towards him.

The bathroom door opens and three black guys step inside, all of them with muscles, tattoos and gold chains and grilles. "This is a private party," you tell them, your fist cocked and ready to hit Ramone again.

"That's okay, we got an invitation," the leader of the three says. He then looks at LT and nods. "What up, LT?"

"What it do, Top Floor?" LT responds.

"Everything it supposed to," he says flashing his gold plated mouth. He looks at you and asks, "What's your beef with my man, here?"

"It's personal," you say.

"Well I've got business with him," Top Floor tells you. "Maybe we can work something out."

> If you tell Top Floor and his buddies to take a hike, go to Scene 105.
> If you decide to listen to what Top Floor has to say, go to Scene 106.

You and LT sneak up to the construction site which consists of half a dozen town homes that were framed but never finished. The van and Charger are parked in front of an open garage, both vehicles empty. You hear voices inside the garage and you motion LT to cover the other side of the van as you creep towards the front bumper for a closer look with your gun in hand.

"You see the product," the gangbanger known as Top Floor says, "now let's see the money."

"Hold up, Dawg," Ramone says to him, "I gotta test it first."

"You can test it while I count the cheddar."

"What, you don't trust me?" Ramone says and then tosses Top Floor an envelope stuffed with cash. Ramone takes a glass pipe out of his pocket and then picks up a shard of meth out of the cooler in front of him. He puts it in the pipe and sets flame beneath the glass bubble.

Top Floor fingers through the money in the envelope and then he nods his head to the two thugs that are standing with their backs to you. One of them lifts up the back of his shirt and reaches for a gun in the waistband at the back of his pants.

"Hey, this shit ain't cracking back," Ramone says, his attention on the glass pipe and lighter in his hands. "This dope is junk."

> If you stay still and let Ramone get popped, go to Scene 107.
> If you help Ramone, go to Scene 108.

You and LT hang tight in his Suburban and watch the two vehicles. Five minutes later you see a single flash of light bounce off the woodwork of the construction site followed by the sound of a gunshot. You grip the gun in your hand and look at LT. He shrugs his shoulders.

The three black guys come out of the shadows and get back in their vehicles and casually drive off.

"I didn't see Ramone with them," LT says.

"Drive down to the site," you tell him.

He parks the Suburban in front of a garage of a partially constructed town home. The headlights of the SUV illuminate the crumpled figure of Ramone on the garage floor. You hop out to check what you already suspect: he's dead with a bullet to the back of the head. You see that all his jewelry has been taken so you know there's no sense checking his pockets.

Getting back in the truck you tell LT to drop you off at home. You're pissed at yourself for not being more proactive and now you're out a serious chunk of cash. You chalk it up to a lesson learned the hard way and tell yourself that tomorrow is another day.

THE END

"Are you just going to sit there and enjoy the ride or are you going to get some shots off at those motherfuckers?" Tony asks you.

You smile and say, "I always did enjoy playing GTA." You lean out the window and blast off a few rounds from the big .44. The cop cars back off, one of them smoking and coming to a stop.

Sirens can be heard in every direction. "At least they're not on our ass," Tony says.

"That's why," you reply and point to the sky where a police helicopter is tailing you.

"Not a problem. Watch this," Tony says and veers the Cadillac across a freeway and weaving in and out of a couple of cross streets. Surprisingly you see the helicopter veer off and give up the chase.

"How the hell did you do that?"

"We're near the airport. It'll take them a few minutes to clear the airspace."

There are still plenty of sirens to be heard and you can see flashing lights a couple hundred yards behind you.

"Reach under the seat," Tony says. "There should be a couple metal hooks under there."

You pull them out and ask what they're for. Tony smiles as he stops the car in the middle of an intersection. He hops out with one of the hooks and tells you to help him. With the hooks you both lift a heavy sewer manhole cover. You go to grab the loot from the car but a cop car smashes into it, sending it spinning across the intersection.

> If you run to the car to get your robbery proceeds, go to Scene 109.
> If you drop down into the manhole without the loot, go to Scene 110.

Paper currency of every denomination is sticking to your and Noelle's sweaty bodies as you fuck her atop a bed that is covered in money. "Oh yes! Oh yes!" she cries out as your thrusting quickens and her pussy pulsates. "Oh my fucking god yes!" You let loose in her as her body vibrates beneath you and her fingernails dig into your back.

A little later, after having eaten room service you ordered to the hotel suite, Noelle is sorting and counting the money from your latest heist.

"Thirty two thousand, seven hundred and six dollars," she says with a smile. "Not counting the fifty we gave to room service."

"Not a bad day's work," you say.

"I want more. I want to see six figures."

"We've practically made that between the jewelry store and theater."

"Maybe total," she says. "But I want six figures each."

"For what?"

"For whatever I want. A car, a condo, shoes. A girl has needs."

"Be careful," you tell her. "Greed can be dangerous. How about we hit the tropics for some fun and sun?"

"But I have needs and wants," Noelle says as she approaches you on the couch and opens your robe. "Surely you can think of another big job," she says, emphasizing big by grabbing your cock which immediately hardens. She slides her sweet, warm mouth over you.

You tilt your head back and say you might be able to come up with something.

> If you plan another big heist with Noelle, go to Scene 111.
> If you tell her you think better on vacation, go to Scene 62.

You're sitting at a table in the far back corner of Shaggy's, Chaz in a chair next to you, a couple of drinks in front of you.

"Almost thirty-five grand apiece," you say and hand Chaz a thick envelope. "I've got Rocco's here as well."

"Didn't you watch the news?" Chaz asks.

"No. Why?"

"Rocco didn't make it."

"What about the hostage?"

"She fell in love with me. Stockholm Syndrome. We're heading to the Bahamas tomorrow." Chaz laughs at the look on your face. "I'm fucking with you. I dumped her in a backyard. She's fine."

"What do we do with Rocco's cut?" you ask.

"What do you mean what do we do with it? We fucking split it."

"Did he have family?"

"None that ever gave a shit about him. Except maybe his aunt who would put money on his books when he was in jail."

"How about we take fifteen each and we'll give her the left over five?" you suggest.

"I don't know," the greedy bastard says.

"Consider it good criminal karma."

"Yeah, alright. Maybe then she'll put money on our books if we ever end up back inside," Chaz says.

"That's what I like about you, always thinking positive. Let's celebrate with another drink."

THE END

You hide out in a dumpy motel on the outskirts of the city. Watching the news as you count the money you learn that the bank teller was found relatively unharmed in a backyard. Two of the bank robbers escaped and one was killed in a shootout after a standoff in an apartment building. You wonder if it was Rocco or Chaz, because if it was the latter you're good to go with the money because you hardly know Rocco and he surely doesn't know you.

You order Domino's and keep watching the news and eventually learn it was Rocco who was killed. The police and FBI are following leads on the Trump bandits. There's no reason to stick around, so you decide to take the almost hundred and five thousand dollars and go on a little road trip.

Back at your place you quickly pack a suitcase. You know it was stupid to come back but you really wanted your phone and your computer. As you rush out your front door you hear what you thought was a car backfire and then you're suddenly flying backwards as if you'd been swatted in the chest with a baseball bat. You land hard on your back and your chest feels hot and wet and you can't breathe.

You look down at the blood bubbling up from your shirt. A shadow washes over you and you look up to see Donald Trump holding a sawed off shotgun. "You're fired," he says and walks off with your suitcase full of cash.

THE END

The kid gives you a good idea and you drive back to your place to pick up a few needed items and then return to the house in the hood. This time you pull up right in front of the house. You step out of the car and straighten the blue blazer you're wearing, the .38 in the shoulder holster feeling bulky beneath your armpit.

Glancing around the neighborhood everyone seems to be going about their day as normal. Nobody is specifically watching you but you know you're on their radar, everybody alert to Five-oh being on the block. You walk up the front steps and rap heavily on the door, your 'cop knock.'

After a moment there's a man's voice from the other side of the door. "Who is it?"

"Police," you say with plenty of bass in your voice. "Open the door please."

You hear the deadbolt being disengaged and the door opens. A man of about seventy peeps out the half opened door. He's wearing a purple sweater vest and reminds you of Mister Rogers.

"I'm Detective Kirvenstitch," you tell him as you hold up a gold badge in a leather wallet. "I need to ask you some questions."

"What's this about?" the old man asks.

"If we can step inside I'll explain."

"Do you have a search warrant?"

"Don't make this hard on yourself. You can let me in or you can come downtown with me."

The old man shakes his head. "You can't come in without a warrant, and I'm not going downtown without a lawyer."

> If you pull your gun and force your way in, go to Scene 112.
> If you leave and continue staking out his place, go to Scene 92.

Night falls as you continue watching the home from down the block. The neighborhood becomes more lively with groups of thuggish young black men moving around. There's loud music, yelling, an occasional gunshot and the squealing of tires.

There's a thump and the car bounces slightly. You look in the rearview mirror to see a black teenager sitting on the trunk of the car while talking and laughing with two other black tattooed teens standing on the sidewalk. You don't think they're aware of you in the vehicle and you don't care if the car gets scratched or dented because it's only a rental.

Lights are on in the house you've been watching, but there has been no movement seen, no one coming or going. You're beginning to feel like this might be a waste of time.

"Hey Joe, there's someone in that car," comes a voice from the sidewalk.

"What the fuck. We got us a peeping Tom," says another voice as bodies crowd closer to your vehicle. A few more thugs from across the street walk towards the car.

You put the driver's side window down and say, "Get the fuck away from the car! This is police business."

"Shit, man, you ain't no cop. They ain't stupid enough to come around here after dark, and especially not riding solo."

Before you can reach for a weapon, a fist hits you in the side of the face and other hands are grabbing you and dragging you out of the car through the open window. You're given a beat down in the middle of the street, stripped of all your valuables and your rental car is stolen. Eventually somebody calls an ambulance and you're carried away.

THE END

With barely a second thought you punch Beth in the back of the head, just behind her right ear. She collapses to the dirty barn floor like a puppet whose strings have been cut. You don't feel bad for her because you figure it's her own fault for being stupid enough to trust some guy she doesn't even know at a random house party.

You find her keys and drive off with the truck, unload the weed at your place and dump the truck on the other side of town. Within a week you have sold all of the pot and netted yourself over a hundred grand, all profit.

A couple of your customers beg for more. "If you can get more of that Purple Dragon or the Denver Girl Scout Cookies, we'll buy it all."

You take a trip to the Mile High City with all your cash with the expectation to pick up seventy to eighty pounds and the next time a hundred plus. You figure within a few months you'll be able to reach the benchmark of one million dollars and call it quits.

What you didn't figure was that Purple Dragon was a rare strain produced by only two growers, one of whom is Beth's father and the other an ex-Navy SEAL that served with her father in Desert Storm. Neither of them are too happy about what happened to Beth and you're never seen or heard from again.

THE END

Within a week you've managed to help her get rid of all of the weed and netted yourself ten grand in profits.

"My guys really like that Purple Dragon," you tell her. "They'll take as much as we can get them."

Beth smiles and says, "That is a bomb strain and I've got the only connect to who grows it. I'll have us another fifty pounds next week."

She follows through and you do your part and find another ten grand in your pocket. You're pretty happy pulling in twenty grand a month working with Beth which involves almost no work at all as the weed practically sells itself.

You get your ride fixed, buy a few more electronics for your home, and find yourself going out to more nicer restaurants. Life is good and all is smooth until one of your boys gets popped, sets you up and you find yourself in the hands of the DEA.

Agent Burhole tells you, "We don't care about you. Just tell us who is bringing in the Purple Dragon and you walk free and clear."

> If you give them Beth, go to Scene 113.
> If you lawyer up, go to Scene 114.

"I don't even know why I'm doing this," you mutter to yourself as you untie Molly.

"Because you think I'm sexy and secretly want to fuck me," she says and gives you a kiss on the cheek.

"Yeah, that's probably it," you say as you shake your head. Of course the prospect of half a million dollars in diamonds has its allure as well.

Your first stop is a Wal-Mart where you run inside and purchase a jogging outfit for Molly and an aluminum baseball bat for yourself.

"It's just an old Chinese guy," Molly explained to you, "and since he just got off the plane you know he can't be armed. All you'll have to do is threaten him and I'm sure he'll give up the briefcase."

At the airport Molly instructs you that the guy drives a light colored Mercedes and it's on the fifth floor of the parking garage. You find three cars, two white and one silver, that could be the target's.

You park as close to the elevators as you can and look at your watch - the plane should be landing in ten minutes. As you get out of the van Molly asks, "What do you want me to do?"

"Just sit tight, I got this," you tell her as you walk away with the baseball bat at your side.

You hide in the shadows and watch the elevators until you see the balding, gray haired Chinese man who can't weigh more than a buck twenty.

> If you confront him with the baseball bat, go to Scene 115.
> If you sneak up behind him and hit him in the head, go to Scene 116.

You shake your head no and get in the driver's seat.

"Aw, come on," Molly says. "You're not seriously going to pass on all that money, are you? Are you? Come on! Untie me at least. I'll do anything. I'll suck your dick."

"Isn't that how you got yourself in this trouble in the first place?" you ask.

You ignore her begging and pleading and bring her back to your cousin Will as instructed. He thanks you and mentions hearing that your ride got smashed up. "Keep the van for a few days and I'll send someone by with a flatbed to pick up your car tomorrow. I've got to keep you mobile just in case I need you again."

"Thanks, cuz," you tell him.

"That's what family's about."

As you drive home you contemplate which of your lady friends you can call and take for a ride in the back of the van.

THE END

You and Ashley agree on a price tag of a hundred grand and she assures you she can have the money for you next week. You know she's good for it.

The Porsche 911 is red with black pin striping and drives like a dream. Maybe you should get yourself one with the money from the hit. From the glove box you pull out a chrome .45 semi-automatic with pearl grips loaded with hollow points: a perfect person killing machine.

The church is located on the south side of town on the edge of a low income neighborhood. It's a quarter to ten and there are four other cars in the parking lot. You back the Porsche in beside a blue Honda Civic at the back of the lot. You keep the motor running, hit the lights off and wait.

At about five minutes after ten, half a dozen people exit the church from a side door and into the parking lot. If you had to guess you'd say it was a gathering of A.A. attendees, but none of them looks like a minister. Three of the people get in two of the cars and the other three exit the parking lot on foot. You watch the two cars leave and wait.

Five minutes later you see a heavy set man with slicked back grey hair exit the church along with a skinny female in jeans and a Metallica t-shirt. The man turns and locks up the church and then walks the female to the Pontiac Grand Prix by the door. They talk for a moment and then she drives off and he stands in place until she leaves the parking lot.

The minister turns and begins walking toward the Honda that you're parked next to. He pulls a set of keys from his pocket and drops them, seemingly oblivious to the Porsche you're sitting in parked fifteen feet away.

> If you try to run him over with the car, go to Scene 117.
> If you wait for him to approach his car and shoot him, go to Scene 118.

You arrive at the minister's home well before ten o'clock, thinking of how you're going to spend the hundred grand that Ashley promised would be in your hands next week. You park the car a block away and walk casually up to the small single story home with the detached single car garage. You wonder how this guy got his hooks into Ashley's mom who is worth millions.

The place has no alarm and once you jimmy the back door and go inside you see why: there's nothing worth stealing. One thing of interest that you do find is a bundle of scented love letters in a desk drawer addressed to Brandon and signed by Ashley. You can't imagine why in the world Ashley was writing love letters to the minister, a couple of them including selfies of Ashley in sexy lingerie.

You wait in the dark for the minister to arrive home, hiding in the corner behind the front door. When Brandon walks in you put the gun to the back of his head and tell him not to turn on the lights.

"Ashley sent you to kill me, didn't she?" the minister asks calmly.

> If you answer with the pull of a trigger, go to Scene 119.
> If you're more curious to know why, go to Scene 120.

"You fucking bastard!" Ashley screams and you turn around in time to catch a knife in the chest. Your first thought is, where in the hell did that come from? Your second thought, as she pulls it out and sticks it back in you is, this really hurts.

You fall to your knees as she screams and continues to stab you. "You're just like all the others!" she cries as your blood spurts everywhere. "I thought you cared about me. I do everything for you. I ask for one little thing and you only use me and abuse me. I just want to be loved like everyone else!"

Your last and final thought as you lay in a puddle of blood is that Ashley doesn't need to hire a killer, she can do it just fine by herself.

THE END

"You got balls," Maggot says, "and I respect that."

He reaches into a desk drawer and throws you a $10,000 stack of bundled hundreds. "Are you sure you don't want to double that?" he asks.

"No, I'm good," you tell him as you put the money in your pocket and turn to leave.

"Come see me if you want to work again," he says before you leave.

Fat chance, you say to yourself. The dude is too shady and untrustworthy. You've got enough cash now to get your car fixed and then you can think about what you'll do next, but whatever it is will be on your terms and of your own doing because ultimately you are the only person you know you can trust one hundred percent.

THE END

Leroy leads the man who looks kind of like Ben Stiller on heroin to the back of the pretzel truck. You and Stan remain at the front of the truck watching the other two men in front of the Suburban, all of you with guns showing sticking out of your waistbands. After a few minutes Leroy and Ben return and both walk to the Suburban. After a few more minutes Leroy nods to Stan who tosses the truck keys to one of the men. Everybody swaps vehicles and leaves and you're paid ten grand for the night's work.

A week later you again accompany Leroy and Stan in a delivery truck to a warehouse on the other side of the river. The buyers this time are two Asian dudes in a Toyota 4-Runner. One of them examines the merchandise with Leroy while the other mean mugs you and Stan. Leroy then accompanies the guy to the 4-Runner.

"What the fuck is this?" Leroy says angrily.

The guy mean mugging you quickly pulls the gun from his waistband and you and Stan do the same. The other Asian comes around the SUV with a gun to Leroy's head.

"Guns down motherfuckers!" the Asian behind Leroy says.

You look at Leroy and he nods his head. Slowly you and Stan put your guns on the ground and the other Asian quickly snatches them up.

"Nothing personal," one of them says before they get into the two vehicles and drive off.

> If you decide to run and jump on the back of the delivery truck, go to Scene 121.
> If you call Maggot and tell him what happened, go to Scene 122.

"Do exactly as I say if you want to get out of this place alive," you growl into her ear. You push her into the bedroom and tell her to stand still as you pull a silk garment from a dresser drawer and tie it around her eyes as a blindfold. You slip a robe over her naked body and then tie her hands behind her back with a pair of panty hose. You find another pair of panty hose and slip them over your head to disguise your face.

"How much does your husband love you?" you ask Alicia.

"A lot," she replies.

"We're about to find out."

When you hear the garage door opening you rush to the bathroom and turn on the faucet on the tub and shut the bathroom door, holding Alicia in a tight grip with the knife to her throat. A couple minutes later Maggot opens the door and says, "Hey baby, are you all wet for--"

His eyes grow wide when he sees you holding his wife and he goes for his gun in his back waistband.

"Don't!" you growl. "Or she dies." The butcher knife is pressed against her neck, a single drop of blood rolling down her pale flesh.

Maggot freezes and says, "If you hurt her, I'll kill you."

"I'm already dead," you say and pull Alicia's hair to make her squeal.

"Okay, okay, don't hurt her."

"Set your gun on the floor, slowly."

You snatch up his gun and push his wife towards him. You make him open the safe and then tie the two of them to a kitchen chair before leaving with over six figures in dope and cash.

"I'll find you!" Maggot yells as you leave.

Maybe, maybe not, but you're living it up for now.

THE END

"Please don't hurt me," Alicia begs. "I'll do anything."

You hold the knife to her throat and slide your hand slowly down the front of her naked body, cupping her voluptuous breast and then sliding your hand over her smooth tummy and feeling the warmth between her legs. The hardness in your pants rubs against her bare ass pressed against you.

You guide her to the bedroom and push her face down on the bed and tell her not to move. You fumble with your pants, getting them undone while still holding onto the butcher knife. Your cock is rock hard and dripping with excitement as you stand beside the bed looking at the naked beauty lying on her stomach.

"Spread your legs," you tell her breathlessly. "Wider."

She does as she's told and your mouth waters at the sight.

You take a step forward and hear a clicking sound. You look down, wondering if you stepped on something, but then realize too late that the sound came from behind you. You slowly look over your shoulder to see Maggot standing there with a large gun to your head.

Fifteen minutes later your hands are tied together and you're hanging from a rafter in the garage. Tears pour down your face and blood pours down your thighs as your severed penis lies on the concrete below you. Alicia stands behind you with the bloody butcher knife while Maggot watches from the side with gun in hand. You wish he would shoot you.

Instead, Alicia says, "Spread your legs. Wider."

THE END

"I need you to take my girls to their appointments," Lil Taco says.

"So you want me to be a pimp?" you ask.

"Naw dawg, I'm the pimp. You just the driver. Maybe someday you get your own ho's and you can be a pimp, too."

He loans you a car to use until you get your ride fixed. Your first run is taking a girl named Erica to a hotel downtown. You figure her name is about as real as her tits and though her body is smoking hot, you don't care for her short hair and shitty attitude.

"Do you want me to come up with you?" you ask.

"No. Stay here. I'll be down in an hour."

Your next run that same night is taking a short, sweet girl-next-door type named Bambi to a motel near the airport. She returns to the car after forty minutes and you notice she's trying to hide tears and when she gets in there's pain on her face when she sits down.

"Are you okay?" you ask. She nods her head but doesn't look at you. "Did that guy hurt you?"

"Sometimes that's what they pay for," she says quietly.

"Is that what you wanted?"

"Do you think this job is what I wanted?"

"What did he do to you?"

"It doesn't matter," she says, wiping away her tears. "We've got to be across town for my next trick in an hour. Can we just go?"

> If you drive her to her next appointment, go to Scene 123.
> If you instead go and knock on the motel door, go to Scene 124.

"Ramone is temporarily closed for business," you tell Top Floor and his two cronies. "This doesn't concern you. But if you want to change that..." you say pulling your shirt up and showing the gun in your waistband.

The three black guys look to LT who also lifts his shirt and puts his hand near the gun in his waistband.

"Another time then maybe," Top Floor says and the three guys slowly back out of the bathroom.

"Aw man, you fucked up my deal," Ramone whines.

"And you fucked up your momma's pussy when you were born," you tell the lowlife at your feet. "Now empty your pockets or I'm going to have LT dunk you in this shit clogged toilet that smells as bad as your breath."

You pull five grand in cash off of Ramone as well as all his jewelry which ends up being worth another three.

"We cool now?" Ramone asks.

"We are," you say, looking at LT, "but you never will be."

You and LT leave the bar, ignoring Ramone's plea for twenty dollars so he can at least get a taxi.

You keep six grand and give the other two to LT for his time and troubles. You decide it best not to lend anyone else any money for a while.

THE END

"What was your business with Ramone?" you ask Top Floor.

"Five stacks worth of crystal," Top Floor answers.

You look at Ramone and ask him, "You got the five G's on you?"

"C'mon, man," he says. "I told you I'll have ten for you next week. This is my deal."

"Give me the fucking money before I drown you in this toilet," you tell him. He reluctantly hands over the cash.

"The shit is pure," Top Floor tells you. "You can double or triple your money depending on how you cut it."

"Let's see it."

"It's close by."

> If you say "No thanks" and keep the cash, go to Scene 125.
> If you and LT go to check out the dope, go to Scene 126.

You figure that Ramone is a fool and gets what he deserves. In the jungle, whether of the trees or concrete, it's survival of the fittest. Maybe if he hadn't tried to punk you out of the money he owed you, you would have been more inclined to help him.

You watch as the gangbanger points his gun at Ramone and shoots him in the face, the body collapsing to the garage floor lifeless. The other gangbanger bends down and goes through Ramone's pockets and removes all of his jewelry.

Top Floor begins to put the envelope of money in his pocket, but seeing as Ramone owed you, you figure that money is rightfully yours. You step out from behind the van with your gun pointed at Top Floor and LT follows your lead with his gun trained on the other two.

"That money belongs to me," you say.

The sound of your voice scares the shit out of the three men, causing them to jump and go for their guns. Before you can say another word, everyone is firing their guns and diving for cover. Ten rounds are fired in the next two seconds, the barrel flashes blinding in the darkness, and then all is quiet except for the ringing in your ears.

You check your body to make sure you haven't been shot and then call out to LT. "Are any of them still alive?" You're pretty sure you hit Top Floor and possibly one of the others. LT doesn't respond and there's no noise coming from the garage. Cautiously you poke your head out and see two bodies on the ground; it's the two gangbangers, dead. Next you find LT with a bullet hole through his left eye, and Top Floor is dead with two rounds to the chest. You get the money, five G's, and then quickly empty everyone's pockets before making your escape. You're content that the most important person made it out alive: you.

THE END

You rush from your hiding spot and put a gun to the back of the head of the gangbanger that was drawing his. "Don't even think about it!" you growl.

The sound of your voice scares the shit out of everyone in the garage and Top Floor and the other gangbanger go for their guns.

"Don't do it!" LT yells, covering them with his gun.

Top Floor looks at Ramone and says, "You set us up. You're a dead man!"

"I didn't set shit up," Ramone says. "Besides, you were going to rip me off." He goes over to Top Floor and snatches the envelope of money from his hands. You in turn snatch the envelope from Ramone's hands. "Hey!" he says.

"Fuck you. That's my money," you tell Ramone.

"You're still a dead man, Ramone," Top Floor says.

"What?" Ramone says and snatches the gun out of Top Floor's waistband and points it at his head. "Who's the dead man?"

"Do it, punk," Top Floor tells him.

Ramone looks over his shoulder at you with a grin, but whether it's to show off or seek your approval you're not sure.

Top Floor snatches the gun and he and Ramone struggle with it, thrashing around the garage. You and LT keep your guns on the two gangbangers who look anxious and jumpy. The gun goes off that Top Floor and Ramone are fighting for and you feel a burning sensation in your left shoulder.

At the sound of gunfire, the two gangbangers dive for cover and you and LT fall back behind the van.

"Let's get the fuck out of here," LT says and he helps you back to his Suburban. At least you got your money, though most will go for surgery and drugs to medicate the pain.

THE END

"What the fuck are you doing?" Tony yells at you as you take off running across the intersection.

"Cover me!" you yell. You hear the sounds of gunshots pinging into the police car twenty feet away. The Cadillac is smashed up against a telephone pole and you reach into the car to grab the two gym bags. When you turn around two more cop cars have screeched to a stop in the intersection, cops swinging open their car doors.

"Oh fuck!" you say. You look to the open manhole cover twenty feet away and see that Tony has already dropped down and disappeared.

You make a run for it, firing off the last rounds of the .44 before throwing it aside and grabbing your other gun. The cops return fire and suddenly you're sliding across the asphalt as one of your legs gives out from being hit by a bullet.

"Drop your gun!" a police officer yells from behind his car. More cop cars are screeching to a halt from every direction.

"Kiss my ass!" you yell and fire off some rounds from your handgun as you crawl towards the manhole opening.

The cops open fire and you feel a couple pin pricks of pain before your body shuts down and goes numb. Your last thought is that at least you probably distracted the cops long enough for Tony to get away. A lot of good that did you as you die bleeding in the street.

THE END

Both you and Tony know that no amount of money is worth your freedom or your lives, so you drop down into the manhole after him. The tunnel under the street is about four feet in diameter and you have to crouch to move through it.

"Do you know where you're going?" you ask.

"Anywhere is better that where we just were," he says.

You come to a four way intersection and Tony goes to the left and you follow after him.

"All I know," he says, "is that a cop would have to be crazy to try to follow us in here without backup and there's no way they can cover the hundreds of exit points across the city."

The two of you zigzag through the underground tunnels, a couple times coming to large tunnels that you can fully stand up in. After about twenty minutes of running, he chooses a ladder to climb and pushes the manhole cover out of the way once he's certain there's no traffic going by overhead.

You find yourself in the middle of a quiet, run down neighborhood. Plenty of sirens can be heard in the distance, as well as a couple of helicopters.

"We should probably split up," you say.

"I was thinking the same thing," Tony replies.

"Good luck."

"You too. Let's try it again sometime."

"You know it," you say before you both run off in different directions.

THE END

"Don't you fucking move!" screams Noelle as she waves a handgun around the office of the bingo hall. You're both dressed in black and wearing ski masks and it's almost midnight when you rush through a back door and kick in the office door to find three employees counting money.

"Money in the bag!" you yell, tossing a duffel bag onto the table while wielding a sawed off shotgun. All three of the employees comply. They're each in their sixties, one man and two women, and all look scared out of their minds.

"Jesus is going to punish you," one of the ladies says to Noelle.

"What?" Noelle says moving toward the lady, her gun pointed in front of her.

"I said--"

"I heard you. How about you tell him I'm going to be awhile."

"No!" you yell, but it's too late as Noelle pulls the trigger and the gun bucks in her hand and half the lady's head is blown away.

"Anyone else with comments?" Noelle asks wildly.

You barely make it back to your hotel room before Noelle is tearing off your clothes and can't get enough of your cock in her mouth and pussy. After you blow your wad she goes on about how thrilling the night was and she can't wait to do it again and she's trying to get you aroused because she can't wait to do that again, too.

She's becoming a fucking killing machine and you know it's only a matter of time until her actions get you hemmed up. You realize you're going to have to get away from her soon before she gets you killed or you end up having to kill her. You're a fool if you stay with her and yet the pussy is so damn good, maybe worth dying for.

THE END

"Here's my warrant right here, old man," you say and pull your gun, sticking it in his face. You follow as he steps backward into the house.

"I wouldn't do that if I were you," the Mister Rogers look alike says.

"Well you're not me, neighbor. I'm the one with the gun. Now where's the package that was delivered here?"

"Louise doesn't like guns," the man tells you.

"What? Who the fuck is Louise? I don't care what--" you stop ranting as you hear a low growl to your right. You glance over to see a German shepherd with her teeth bared less than six feet away.

"You better call off that dog," you tell the man.

"And Thelma doesn't care for men," the man says staring at you casually.

To your left is growling from another German shepherd, teeth bared and moving towards you. Before you can turn your gun on Thelma, Louise has already leaped and clamped onto your forearm. You scream and then Thelma is burying her teeth into your thigh.

"Okay, okay!" you cry out as your gun drops to the floor. "I'll go, I'll leave. I'm sorry."

"It's a little late for that...neighbor. The girls want to play."

You become a tug of war toy between the two dogs who begin to tear you to pieces.

THE END

The DEA agent tells you that with your criminal record you'll be looking at twenty years, but with your cooperation in taking down Beth he assures you that you'll walk free and clear. Maybe you'd think differently if you'd known Beth for a number of years or if she was family or something, but you really hardly know the girl and you're not about to take the chance of sitting in prison for her.

You tell the agents what they want to know and once they arrest Beth you have to take the stand and testify against her. True to Agent Burhole's word, you don't face any charges and you walk free and clear of the courthouse once the trial is finished.

A block from the courthouse two scary looking dudes approach you and one of them flashes a gun with a silencer attached. Both guys are in their fifties, the one who flashed the gun is wearing a stocking cap, the other guy is bald and both look like their faces were chiseled from granite blocks.

"Come with us," the bald guy says.

You feel like you have little choice and as you walk down the sidewalk between them you say, "I don't know you. I think you've got the wrong guy."

"You talk too much," the bald man says as he stops next to a cargo van and slides open the side door, "especially in the courtroom."

"What? Who are you?" you ask.

"I'm Beth's father. Now get in the van."

"No way! I'm not--" your words are cut short by the two bullets that enter the back of your skull and propel your body into the van.

THE END

You tell the agent you don't know what he's talking about and that you want a lawyer. You've been making good money and can afford a decent attorney, but to your surprise one of the city's best drug case attorneys shows up to represent you and tells you that all his fees are already being covered. You know who covered his fees, the same person who pays your bail.

"Thanks," you tell Beth as soon as you're out of jail.

"Thanks for not ratting on me," she says.

"That's not my style."

"The attorney is pretty sure he can get you probation and worst case would possibly be a year in the workhouse."

"Don't do the crime if you can't do the time," you say.

"If you end up with any time," she tells you, "you won't have to worry about your books ever being empty."

"Thanks."

"Of course if the associate of yours that set you up doesn't make it to court, you walk for sure."

"Very true. He's obviously suicidal to have done what he did."

"And it's astonishing how many people go missing every day."

"Yes it is," you say thinking about how you're going to assure that you stay out of jail.

THE END

You step out of the shadows wielding the baseball bat menacingly at the small Chinese man. "Give me the briefcase and you won't get hurt," you tell him.

"No," he answers, standing still and staring at you.

"Wrong answer," you say and swing the bat at his head.

The old man ducks the swinging bat effortlessly and then he's moving quickly - but towards you, not away from you. His hands and feet are a blur but the pain is like strikes of lightening to your chest, groin, head as well as your arms and legs as you uselessly attempt to block the blows. Your bones snap and you're left lying in a bleeding heap on the cold concrete, in more pain than you've ever felt in your life.

The old man disappears and you cling to consciousness hoping that Molly will show up because you don't think you can stand on your own and won't be walking for quite some time.

THE END

You rush up behind the old man and blast him in the back of the head with the baseball bat and he collapses to the pavement like a wet bag of laundry. You grab the briefcase, run to the van and quickly drive off.

"Oh wow, look at these," Molly says after opening the briefcase and scooping up a handful of diamonds. "You did great," she says and gives your thigh a squeeze.

"What's that?" she asks.

"I always get a little excited after a successful job."

"Let's see," she says and begins unzipping your pants. You protest, but not too much as you focus on driving down the freeway. Molly begins sucking your cock, some of the best roadhead you've ever had, and then you're exploding in her mouth and she licks you clean.

Ten minutes later you're dropping the diamonds off with one of your guys who says he'll have the money for you tomorrow. You then take Molly to Will's to tell him the good news.

"You did what!" Will yells.

"They're worth at least four hundred thousand," you tell him.

"I know how much they're worth! That was my guy you hit. I can't fucking believe this. Hell, why not fuck my girl while you're at it?"

You and Molly look at each other and then you quickly say, "I didn't fuck, I mean I wouldn't fuck your girl. I can get the diamonds back."

"You damn well better or heads are going to fly!" Will yells.

You leave and hope your guy hasn't gotten rid of the diamonds yet. You kind of like your head right where it's at.

THE END

You gun the engine and the small sports car shoots forward. The minister raises his head just before the front of the car hits him with a loud thud. His body flies in the air over the Porsche and slams to the pavement behind you as you slam on the brakes. You see the man of the cloth in your rearview mirror moving slowly, trying to get up.

You shift the car into 'Reverse' and stomp the accelerator and hear a satisfying thud and crunch as the car hits the man and then runs over him. Shifting back into first gear, the sports car bounces as the rear tires go over the body. Looking in the sideview mirror you can see by the glow of the brake lights that half of the minister's head is crushed and he won't be getting up ever again.

You take off out of the parking lot and return to Ashley.

> Go to Scene 119.

As the minister walks toward the Honda Civic he slows as he eyes the Porsche that's parked suspiciously close. You can tell he thinks something is wrong and suddenly he takes off running around the backside of the church. You jump out of the sports car and give chase, the gun in your hand.

The minister runs down a small set of steps into a door well. You're fifteen yards away as you raise the gun in your hand but the minister is through the door and inside the church. You rush down the steps and through the doorway, finding yourself in a small storage room with another door that leads to the main area of the church.

Eerie shadows are cast about the church from the street lights coming through the stained glass windows that line the church walls. You hear the sound of movement near the altar and slowly approach, checking each row of pews you pass.

An organ to the right of the altar blares to life and a jolt of fear causes you to pull the trigger and fire a round into the offending instrument. Someone appears in a light behind the altar and you quickly fire again before realizing that you just shot Jesus who's already nailed to a cross. This place is starting to freak you the fuck out and you think maybe it's time to leave, maybe get the minister at his home, or maybe just drop the whole job.

You reach the altar and hear a sound behind you. You spin and face the pews but see nothing. You hear another sound behind you and spin to see a silver cross being swung like a baseball bat at your neck, piercing the flesh on one side and poking out through the other in a fountain of blood. You fall to your knees in front of the minister who still holds the cross. The last words you hear are, "as we forgive those who trespass against us."

THE END

Ashley tells you she'll have your hundred G's the following week after you off the minister. When you show up to collect she only has ten thousand for you.

"This is a little short," you tell her.

"It's the bank's fault," she says, "but it should be cleared up by the end of the week. In the meantime, I've got another job for you to do."

"I'm not doing another job. You haven't even paid me for this one."

"You have to. The cops are snooping around and this person knows about the minister. If the cops get to him it will lead to me and that will lead to you."

"Are you threatening me?" you ask.

"No. I'm just telling you the facts. Come on, what do I need to do to convince you?"

She sees you eye her body up and down and she says, "I won't cheat on my boyfriend, but you can fuck me in the ass if you want."

It turns out that you want. She lifts her dress and slips her panties down and bends over the couch exposing her luscious ass to you. You immediately become hard and drop your pants. You slather your cock up with saliva and then grip Ashley's ass cheeks, spreading them apart and exposing her chocolate starfish. She moans as you push slowly into her tight asshole that grips you like a velvet vice. Your hands grip her hips and soon you're pounding in and out of her and she's crying out in joyous pain until you're exploding inside her.

You enjoy fucking her just as you're sure she enjoys fucking you by holding the murder over your head and making you do her bidding. You'll play her game for now but you know eventually you'll have to get something on her or take her out if want to protect yourself.

THE END

"She's crazy," the minister says standing deathly still in the dark. "She said if she can't have me, then nobody can. I can show you love letters that she has continued to give to me, putting them in my house, on my car, in my church."

"Did you and her...?" you ask, leaving the question open.

"No, never. She would attend my Sunday sermons and sit in the front pews wearing short dresses with nothing on underneath. She even got into my house once and was waiting for me in the bathtub with candles all over."

"Yeah, your security sucks. So why not call the police?"

"And tell them what? That a beautiful, spoiled rich girl is infatuated with me. I'd be laughed out of the precinct. Unless you came with me and told them she hired you to kill me, maybe you could wear a wire or something."

"That will never happen," you tell him.

"No, I didn't think so."

You both stand in silence in the dark. You lower the gun and tell the minister he should think about beefing up his security.

"Bless you," he says, his body trembling in the dark as you slip out the door and leave.

You drop the Porsche off at Ashley's but decide not to see her. You don't know what's going on and don't want to be involved in her craziness. But just in case, you decide to hang onto the gun.

THE END

Without even thinking about it, you run after the delivery truck and jump onto the back. Unfortunately you didn't have time to snatch your gun off the ground, but you figure that's not much of a problem as you slide open the back door of the truck that's filled with weapons. You open a few of the crates until you find what you're looking for.

You wait until the truck rolls to a stop at a stop light and as soon as it starts to roll again you pull the pin on a grenade and drop it into a crate of grenades. You jump out of the back and watch the truck make it about thirty yards down the road until it erupts in a huge explosion that sends an orange fireball into the sky.

Surely Maggot will be pissed about losing the shipment, but not as pissed if you let it go without a fight. At least you didn't let somebody simply punk you out of the shit.

Leroy and Stan are reprimanded for doing nothing and you move a notch closer to running Maggot's empire of drugs and guns.

THE END

"You let them just punk you out of the shipment?" Maggot screams at the three of you once you're back at his place. "None of you put up a fight?"

"They got the drop on us," Leroy says.

"There were three of you and only two of them!"

"They had a gun to my head," Leroy states.

"And?" Maggot hollers, his eyes wild.

"Leroy told us to drop our weapons," Stan says.

"Is that so?"

You and Stan nod your heads. Maggot pulls out a gun and puts it to Leroy's head and says, "The next time someone puts a gun to one of your heads..." He pulls the trigger and the back of Leroy's head explodes in a pink mist. Leroy crumples to the ground. "You fucking waste them!"

You and Stan nod your heads.

"I suggest you take precautions not to find yourselves in that predicament," Maggot says. "Now grab some firepower and let's go see about getting my shit back."

You prepare yourself for a war in the streets.

THE END

Seeing as you're being paid to drive a ho, not be Captain Save-a-Ho, you simply do as you're supposed to and bring Bambi to her next appointment across town.

You end up making a couple hundred dollars for your night's work but you're not sure if it's something you can see yourself doing on the regular.

Maybe it's easier being a pimp and just collecting the money and not having to actually see the girls after each trick and the sadness that seems etched on their faces.

Or maybe you're getting soft in your old age and had better just stick with your day job and stop trying to be a hustler. You don't see much of a future for any of the girls you've been driving and it gets you to thinking about your own future and where it's going.

You keep telling yourself there's something more out there for you. You just hope you find it soon, before it's too late.

THE END

"Where are you going?"

"I'll be right back," you tell Bambi as you get out of the car.

You knock on the motel door and a balding man about your height with an extra spare tire around his belly answers the door. He's wearing a pair of white boxers with pinstripes and a wife beater tank top and in his hand he holds a leather belt.

"What the fuck do you want?" he asks.

You punch him in the mouth and he staggers backwards. You rush into the room and swing at the man again, but he ducks and rams his head into your chest, knocking you onto the bed. Before you can get up the man is swinging the leather belt, the brass belt buckle cutting into your arms as you block the blows.

"You want some of what the bitch got?" he yells and keeps whipping you.

You finally get off the bed and tackle the man into the wall. The two of you begin wrestling, crashing around the room, making a loud ruckus as you beat on each other.

The motel room door flies open and two police officers enter with their guns drawn. You and the man stop fighting, both of you bloody and breathing hard.

One of the officers looks at the man in the boxers and says, "Sergeant, what are you doing here?"

Your jaw drops and the sergeant looks at you and says, "You should have minded your own business. Arrest him!"

THE END

A bird in the hand is worth two in the bush, you tell yourself. There's something about Top Floor and his two cronies that you don't like, your little voice telling you it doesn't feel right and you know it's always good to listen to that inner voice.

"No thanks, I'm good," you tell Top Floor and you and LT leave the bar.

At least you got most of the money owed to you by Ramone and if you get bored sometime you can always go brace Ramone for the rest plus interest.

The five G's will be enough to get your ride fixed and back on the road and tomorrow is a new day for hustling.

THE END

You and LT follow Top Floor and his sidekicks to a garage in a construction site of unfinished town homes. You all get out of your vehicles and Top Floor shows you a small cooler that holds a large plastic bag of what looks to be meth.

"Let's see it," you say.

"Let's see the money," he replies.

You hand him the envelope with cash that you took off Ramone and Top Floor tosses you the cooler.

"Do you have a pipe so we can test this shit?" you ask.

"Jerome," Top Floor says to one of his guys, "go get that piece out of the car."

You figure if the stuff is pure like Top Floor said, you can probably triple your money when you cut the shit.

Jerome returns but the piece he's holding turns out to be a sawed-off shotgun.

"What the fuck is this?" you say.

Top Floor snatches the cooler out of your hands and says, "We figure if you're friends of Ramone's then you're probably as stupid as him, too. The only difference is I think we'll let you live."

"If you think you're going to rip me off and walk the streets without looking over your shoulder, you've got another thing coming," you tell him.

"Okay," Top Floor says and nods his head.

The last thing you hear is the roar of the shotgun before your world ends.

THE END

In Me I Trust FAQ

Q: I keep dying all the time.
A: That isn't a question. Obviously you keep making bad decisions.

Q: Are there any happy endings when you're a gangster?
A: There are 15 happy endings, 24 bad endings and 7 that are okay
   depending on your outlook.

Q: Are any of the scenarios in the book based on real life events?
A: No, it's a fucking book you moron. None of the characters or crimes
   are based on reality.

Q: This book has given me some good ideas and I was thinking of
   committing one of the crimes for real.
A: Again, not a question. And it's a very ignorant statement that will
   likely land you in prison beside the author.

Q: I'm all about the ladies. How many different ones can I have sex with
   in this book?
A: If you play your cards right - or wrong - there are eight different
   women you could have sex with, some more than once.

Q: I want to commit as much criminal activity as possible in this book.
   How do I know when I've done it all?
A: The following is a checklist of criminal endeavors that can be found
   in this book:

Murder

Assault

Kidnapping

Burglary

- Home
- Business

☐ Robbery

- Bank
- Jewelry Store
- Bingo Hall

- Drug Dealer
- Diamond Courier

☐ Home Invasion

☐ Gun Running

☐ Drug Running

- Distribution of Marijuana
- Distribution of Methamphetamine

☐ Impersonating a Police Officer

☐ Human Trafficking

☐ Murder for Hire

☐ Auto Theft

☐ Fleeing a Police Officer

About the Author

D. Mann has spent more than half his adult life in state and federal prisons due to less than optimal decisions. You may contact the author through Deviant Ways Publications.

Follow Deviant Ways Publications for information and updates on more exciting reads at:

www.DeviantWaysPublications.com

www.Facebook.com/Deviant.Ways.Publications/

Deviant Ways Publications
PO Box 94
Montrose, MN 55363
www.DeviantWaysPublications.com

Duncan just came into a whole bunch of cash.

Unfortunately, the folks who printed it want it back!

Midlife crisis with a backpack full of money, what's one to do? ROAD TRIP!

Chasing the dream while being chased has never been more fun - unless you get caught by the people chasing you! Then there's the strippers, the feds... Everyone wanting to take:

<u>The Money Shot</u>